Courage

Courage

A NOVEL
OF THE SEA

Alan Littell

THOMAS DUNNE BOOKS
ST. MARTIN'S PRESS ≈ NEW YORK

This is a work of fiction. All of the characters, organizations, and events portrayed in this novel are either products of the author's imagination or are used fictitiously.

THOMAS DUNNE BOOKS.
An imprint of St. Martin's Press.

Library of Congress Cataloging-in-Publication Data

Littell, Alan.

Courage / Alan Littell. — 1st ed.

p. cm.

ISBN-13: 978-0-312-38436-4

ISBN-10: 0-312-38436-X

1. Courage—Fiction.   2. North Atlantic Region—Fiction.   I. Title.

PS3612.I869C68   2008

813'.6—dc22

2008025781

First published in the United States by Brillig Press, Inc.

First St. Martin's Press Edition: December 2008

10   9   8   7   6   5   4   3   2   1

For Caroline

I remember my youth…the feeling that I could last
forever, outlast the sea, the earth, and all men; the
deceitful feeling that lures us on…to vain effort.

—Joseph Conrad

Courage is no good…
Being brave
Lets no one off the grave,
Death is no different whined at than withstood.

—Philip Larkin

For a time now he had been thinking about the vessel's deep, rapid roll.

Part One

September — December 1949

*O*n the tramp's bridge a man stood wedged against the rolling between the starboard rail and the repeater compass. He was tall, with gray hair and a gaunt face—it wore a faintly abstracted expression—and he sucked at the dottle of a dead pipe as he watched the long glassy swells of early autumn curl from the north across the sea.

For a time now he had been thinking about the vessel's deep, rapid roll. It was all out of proportion to the state of the sea. The man braced his legs to a sharper toss; he brooded over weights and measures. The problem confounded him. He shipped eight thousand tons in bulk of Newcastle coal. He had computed the lading with care; he bore some of the cargo high, yet the center of gravity defied his meddling. There was the mystery. It remained obdurately low.

The man reworked in his mind a reckoning of buoyancy, gravity, righting moment: the arcana of his trade. Nothing for it but a re-shuffled burden on return passage. He would not have this non-sense in a carrier of uncrated goods. Her stowage was off the mark. She was too bloody stiff. Why, with a heavy sea running she might topple onto her beam like an unbalanced toy. His mind retreated from the notion. Still, no escape from it. The vision intruded: the cant of the deck; worse, the cargo aslide. Fat chance of recovery!

Standing off to the west of Ireland, the ship was brightly painted and pretty to look at in the empty sea. You could tell from her unpit-ted bow plates that she was new from the builder's yard. She was strongly made. She had five holds. She had a nine-cylinder diesel engine, which drove her efficiently at sixteen knots. She had the usual appendages of emergency gear: a powerful sending radio, two commodious lifeboats. Her crew numbered thirty-five, including the man on the bridge, the master, who was called Tyrrel.

At her launching, from one of Scott's old places on the Clyde, the tramp had paused; had hesitated on the tallowed ways as if retarded by a point of friction. (Only later would the Greenock men who had built her—the lofters, platers, shipwrights—remind themselves with the benefit of hindsight that she "widna gae" to sea.) As she floated free a cheer went up. A handsome little ship. Like her prede-cessors Amphion and Patroclus, she was styled by her owners (in the fussy, allegorical way that shipmen had at the time) after a hero of myth: in this instance the noblest of them all. A bottle of wine had shattered against her bows. Her name was Achilles.

1

There was no war that year. There was a lack of cargoes and little shipping.

At summer's end Driscoll joined a rusted and antediluvian freighter, *Ocean Star*, out of New York. The sorry billet was the only one on offer; he signed aboard as third mate. After the first voyage, to Le Havre with half-filled holds, jobs began rotating to men on the beach. Driscoll made one more crossing. Homeward bound, his name appeared on a list radioed from shore.

"You'll pay off in New York," the chief mate said. "The old man will give you a good letter."

"Not much use, is it?"

"All he can do. Look for something ashore."

"There's nothing for me ashore."

The chief mate glanced for a moment over the bridge rail. Brown patches of sargasso weed floated by on the Gulf Stream.

"Hard times," the mate said. He turned away. Driscoll went below and packed his gear.

The ship docked in the rain at the foot of Twenty-third Street. Driscoll walked along cargoes piled high in the dark, dank shed. He went through the customs post and found a pay phone at the head of the pier. For a minute or two he stood listening to the whistles of river craft. All the time he was thinking about his hard luck. He looked at his watch. Nearly six. The light was fading fast. She answered on the third ring. Where in heaven's name was he? North River, just ashore.

Stepping into West Street, he walked with a lurching gait. A taxi drew alongside. Driscoll lifted in two leather suitcases, his sextant box strapped to one of them. His dark hair and fore-head were wet from the rain. He had hollow cheeks and faint lines spreading back from the corners of his eyes. He was of medium height and meager build, a youngish man, not older than thirty. He wore khaki drill and a white shirt, for the day was warm. "Go up Twenty-third to Fifth," he said to the driver. He gave the driver an address on Seventy-seventh Street east of the park.

At Fifth Avenue the cab turned north. Once more Driscoll thought about his hard luck. And now again, her flat as refuge;

she herself as refuge. Intimation of a larger life. Less hedged about than that of the trade of ships. But the notion had not taken root; had not endured the length of his stays ashore.

Through the window of the cab he could see pigeons sheltering under the eaves of rain-stained buildings. The equestrian statue in the square in front of the Plaza Hotel was greened over with verdigris and pigeon droppings. A horse pulling a black carriage struck off smartly into Central Park. An open carriage: two couples laughing in the rain. The coachman wore a red slicker, gleaming. Driscoll thought of Istanbul: after the war.

A small woman. Delicate oval face; hectic coloring. A red cloth bag hung from her shoulder. On the railed platform atop the ship's ladder, one of her feet groped for the first step. It would go no farther. She swayed. She clutched the wire bannister for support. Her eyes darted in fright. Driscoll, the second mate, passing on some errand, caught her arm; gripped both of her hands as she descended backward to the landing stage.

Later in the day he roamed the dim meanders of the covered bazaar. A throng pressed round him. He let himself be carried on the flood: elbowed, pushed. Someone plucked childishly at the back of his sleeve. He turned, surprised.

"I *am* a nuisance."

She pointed, irresolute, impatient.

"It must be the way out. I'm certain I came from that direction."

"No," he said. "Not that way."

He guided her along vaulted passageways, past a lute shop with its fragrant scent of wood shavings; past stalls and shops whose recesses glimmered with brass. They emerged squinting in the sun on the old tentmakers' street and followed the lanes spilling downhill from Süleyman mosque to the spice markets at Eminönü. Along the quays they could see the ferries that plied the harbor east to the breakwater at Harem. On the far side of the Galata Bridge, in Karaköy, a Black Sea steamer for Trabzon was casting off from the Maritime Terminal. Driscoll's ship, the *City of Tampa*—bright gold funnel, dangling accommodation ladder—lay a hawser's length abaft.

Now, crossing the bridge, the metropolis rising in tiers before them, the woman apologized for being so stupid about the ladder. It was inexcusable. But it could not be helped. She had found it impossible to master her fear.

And Driscoll thought: the woman's timidity. Her funk. His own? He admitted it. He pondered old ghosts. They evoked the caprice of fortune. Hauled once from the water choking on oil. Tidied up; sent back to sea—no time then for the niceties. Still, no damage done. As good as new. He might have been immortal. None of it would touch him.

They walked on Istaklal Caddesi. Horse carts and trucks jostled for space. The thoroughfare was pungent with the smell of dung and hot dust. Impulsively the woman grasped Driscoll's hand, for the city unsettled her. Near Taksim Square they entered a hotel. It was high-ceilinged, cool, austere. They drank Tom Collinses on a terrace with a view of the Bosporus. Across the strait, minarets scraped the sky like darts above Üsküdar.

Was it he who proposed they take a room? Perhaps it had been understood. There was some bother about a passport: Driscoll carried a mariner's identity card. The desk clerk wagged a cautionary finger. It would not do. But from her cloth bag the woman, whose name was Isabel Tennant, produced the requisite document, bound in dull green linen, eagle rampant. It was she who signed the register. They were Mr. and Mrs. Tennant that first night, clumsily entwined and instantly asleep, chaste from a surfeit of gin (when he awoke she was gone). And they were Tennant again, in Naples, where she—artist, amateur of the arts—would disembark with her charcoals and sketchbook for excursions to the galleries of Rome and Florence before reboarding in Leghorn; and yet again in the lake country above the Liguri, in the north. And over the years, he drifted into and out of her flat, in New York, when the vessels he sailed in called at that city or at some other port on the East Coast.

The driver stopped in a block of brownstones and tall shade trees. Driscoll went up to Isabel's landing. She stood waiting in the hall.

He bent to kiss her.

"Your shirt is soaked. You had better change. Have you had anything to eat?"

"Is there something to drink?"

"Do you want whiskey?"

"Yes."

In front of him, through the doorway, was a large room. An easel stood next to a window. There were trays of oils and brushes. Paintings were propped in a corner. He could see vistas of rivers, mountains, vineyards, idyllic fields; lanes edged with poplars.

A lace curtain softened the outline of the building opposite and of a tree trunk that was dark with rain. A bed leaned against one wall; a sofa against another. Shelves propped on bricks served as a bookcase, and magazines and newspapers overflowed a footstool. There were three chairs in the room, also a pretty rosewood table. There was a chest of drawers. A door opened onto a narrow passage. A kitchen and bath were at the end of the passage.

He grubbed in his kit for a shirt. Isabel returned from the kitchen with a glass.

"How long will you stay?"

"I don't know. There isn't any work."

He gazed round the room. He seemed puzzled. It was as if he had not seen it before. Here was a reality he could not comprehend. His face was pale with fatigue.

Isabel shook her head in sudden anger. Would he not give it up?

"Damn you, Johnny."

*I*n early October Achilles *discharged her coal at Montreal and made a quick turnaround, with wheat for London. Clearing the Gulf of St. Lawrence, the tramp set a course for the open sea. Captain Tyrrel paced the wheelhouse. With an ocean yet to cross he thought about tides: the London tides. He would fetch the pilot station at Gravesend on the half flood; he was deeply laden and wanted plenty of water under his keel. Then up London River the twenty or so miles to Limehouse Reach, timing his arrival at Millwall for slack water or the first of the ebb.*

London was his and his ship's home port. He lived with a widowed sister in a tidy brick row house off Bishop's Park in the Stevenage Road, miles upriver from the East End grain docks. He had never married. It occurred to him that a sailor was a fool to take a wife. He was a solitary man, a taciturn man. In some other age he would have been a Schoolman. The cloister attracted him. He sought order and continuity. He rummaged obsessively in an idealized English past. He read Stubbs and Maitland on the sanctity of English law. He read Macaulay and the younger Trevelyan, celebrants and elegists of the English countryside. He was fastidious in his person, abstemious in his habits. His sole indulgences were a Heath sextant of uncommonly fine workmanship (engraved silver arc inlaid in brass, the instrument boxed in polished mahogany) and a rack of handsome briars charged with a favored tobacco—Three Nuns—which he crushed to crumbs from tarry coils. The metaphor of the recluse did not cross his mind: he simply fancied the aroma and taste.

As master of his ship, Captain Tyrrel was accustomed to deference and obedience. The sea was his dominion. It was where he ruled. If truth be told, he cared little for London. He disliked the crush of the crowds, the sulphurous stink of coal smoke. The city was an abomination. And he loathed especially, at voyage end, the obligatory interview, on Fenchurch Street, with the line's senior partner, old Shawcross. The man was a tightlipped mercenary who, to his credit, spared no expense in the building of his ships but was singularly parsimonious in the running of them. There would be Shawcross jabbing a finger at entirely unremarkable invoices for stores, fuel, pilotage, port duties. "Indeed, sir, indeed! What possibly could have possessed you? The firm will be in ruin with costs like these!" Inwardly, Captain Tyrrel shrank from the man facing him. He recoiled from the dark oak wainscot surrounding him. The tedium and tyranny of the office suffocated him. Enraged by the rebuke, he would rise, hands trembling (Shawcross in the meantime having summoned from an anteroom another hapless master mariner or chief engineer), and flee to the street.

Still, the captain thought—with Achilles cruising south now of Eastern Shoals, and Cape Race astern—a few days ashore would not be unwelcome. Mind you, he admitted this only to himself. Shawcross be damned!

Achilles worked her way east in damp air patched with fog. It was warm for the season, and the sea, undulating easily, was gray and smooth. Soon the fathometer stylus fell away, tracing a shallow ramp on the chartroom recorder. The stylus leveled at the hundred-fathom mark, then plunged to its stops, signifying the Atlantic deeps. The rollers lengthened. Haze veiled the horizon. Sea and sky merged in a white continuum.

Captain Tyrrel had recalculated the stowage of his ship, apportioning weight yet higher in the 'tween-decks, with the grain, which flows like oil, penned securely in place by temporary wooden bulkheads. He noted with approval the easy rolling under his feet. Achilles rose and dipped to the swell like a floating duck. The stiffness is out, the captain said to himself; we'll see how she does when it comes on to blow. He strode the starboard wing of the bridge, pleased with his command.

At the far end of the wing, a stocky, muscular youth washed paintwork with a bucketful of caustic solution. He had ginger hair and a ruddy face. His hands were blistered from the caustic, which sailors called soogee. He rubbed the paintwork with a rag, then straightened momentarily to look out over the dodger. He liked the way a breath of wind touched his cheek. He liked to watch the sharp *bow cleave the water and turn back a furrow of foam. As the deckboy gazed at the ocean, the chief officer, Mr. Rowe, filled the wheelhouse door.*

"Get on with it," the mate said sternly.

The boy—his name was Joe Corcum—bent to the task. He did not mind. He was happy he had come to sea. Secretly he yearned for officers' braid. From time to time he glanced in awe and admiration at Captain Tyrrel, who, deep in thought, continued his perambulation, remote, aloof, unheeding. Yet the deckboy felt a singular affinity with that magisterial figure. For Joe, too, like the master, was a Londoner, though hardly from the sober precincts west of Whitehall. He was a Thameside tough: with a bit of drink in him, a cheerful brawler. Shadwell and Wapping had been his nursery: the derelict terraces of the Cockney east: a blitzed and broken landscape. He had grown to young manhood prowling the ruins of dockland. And for as long as he could remember, he had loved the river and been drawn to the ships that called there.

Now he would put in his time; sit for his ticket. One day, he was sure, he would be a shipmaster.

2

The next day it was raining still. Harder now. Isabel kept a car in a garage close by. She wished to see the ship he had left. With Driscoll at her side she drove across the city. She turned south at the river. Where the road climbed to an elevated highway the masts and raked funnels of ocean liners came into view. Hatch tents were suspended from the vessels' cargo booms, and pallets laden with freight swung in and out through openings in the canvas cones.

The rain fell. The river was wan. A glimmer of light shone through the windows of a ship's wheelhouse.

"Is that the one?"

"No. Keep going."

Yet he contemplated the light with secret intelligence. He knew the world that lay round it. Beneath its aureole an officer (unseen, surmised) would stand writing at a waist-high desk. Housekeeping details of a ship in port: a note about cargo handling, the loading of bunker fuel. The man would be bareheaded, his badge cap pushed to the edge of the desk. He wore brass-bound blue serge and sturdy black shoes. He would be absorbed in his ledger. He was isolated from humanity: his withdrawal the essence of seafaring. He would hear the solemn ticking of the wheelhouse clock and the chiming of the hour.

There was something about the man (still unseen, still imagined) that Driscoll was unable to grasp. A vital link of understanding. It eluded him. It had to do with rectitude. Driscoll was the man on the bridge. A ship that fed and housed him— there must be more to the matter. Life itself might be the potent sacrifice for this artifice of steel, or was that a romantic illusion? And he thought: in the proper conduct of his profession, was he not a moral man, a man of rectitude? Yet the shore in its corruption and conceit was the nettle that tempted him.

Isabel, concentrating on the road, did not observe his reverie. She could have been far away. She turned in half profile. The sharp line of her jaw tipped upward questioningly. Her beauty dazzled him. In the light without shadows it had a febrile intensity. It was, again, a liberating fantasy of the future. It was also a torment and a warning, for his future would not be divined.

The rain beat against the windshield. He dozed.

"Johnny." Isabel prodded him awake. The booms of a freighter poked at odd angles out of the rain.

"Slow a bit."

The car coasted in gear.

"That's the one," he said.

"Somehow I expected more of you." But the ship was real, proof enough.

Mooring lines drooped from the vessel's bows. A spill of bunker oil, rain pocked and iridescent, awash with planks and dead fish, lapped against the hull. *Ocean Star*: letters rust-white on corroded black.

Driscoll had come to fancy that antique. It was nothing Isabel would fathom, and he was not much closer to the truth of it himself. It needed effort to work through riddles. "There's something to this," he said.

And Isabel, too, mused on his sea life, though with repugnance. The metaphysics of it was beyond her. It was too abstruse. She put it out of mind. She knew only that she was comfortable with him. She cherished him. And she said to herself: I want to keep him.

*T*he heart of mercantile London had the subtle odor of romance about it. There was a scent in the air of foreign places: the sour fragrance of seawrack and river mud, wet hemp and Malay rubber. Commerce had to do with ships and bills of lading. Where Leadenhall Street intersected the ancient thoroughfares of St. Mary Axe and Lime Street, the underwriters of Lloyd's kept their premises. And on St. Mary Axe itself—a gentle crescent ranging northward from the church of St. Andrew Undershaft (whose Maypole once marked the site)—bulked that granite Victorian fortress, No. 24, known to shipmen in all waters as the Baltic: more properly the Baltic Mercantile and Shipping Exchange. The place was a cathedral of sorts. Its god was trade. For in this lofty pavilion of marble pillars and stained-glass alcoves brokers in coal and other commodities came together in grave and sacerdotal parley with brokers in ships to engage transport; and it was here through their surrogates that the astuteness—some would say rapaciousness—of Achilles's owners, Shawcross chief among them, turned a glut of shipping to profitable advantage. The senior partner was a ruthless man. In a time of poor employment he drove down carriage rates to a floor that few of his competitors cared to match. While the tonnage of other houses lay idle, ships of the Shawcross London Line did not want for freight. Indeed, they made their passages with holds abundantly filled. Thus in November, with a new charter offering, Achilles, then at Barry Dock, sailed for the first time to the southern ocean. She carried a cargo of best Welsh coal for Santos and would fetch wheat from the River Plate.

The voyage south was through a dark and endless sea. The ship's steady wake, white and emerald, trailed beneath a clear bright sky. Well south of the Azores the trade winds puffed up out of the northeast, shading the sea to cobalt. The ship went south into the timeless blue and the days stretched without count one into another.

In the ship's logbook appeared few remarks save for the monotonously repetitive record of speed, course, distance run, state of the sea, strength of the wind. Achilles seemed fixed for eternity in the center of a vast blue universe. Each noon the sun stood a few degrees higher on the meridian and the succession of crosses the navigators inscribed on their charts adduced half-believed evidence of progress toward an empty horizon. And at night blue phosphorescence flashed like static electricity in the wash along the bows.

Arriving at Santos late in the month, Achilles discharged her coal. She proceeded in ballast—sea water in deep tanks, slag and

wet sand in the 'tweendecks and lower holds—to the Plate. At Bue-
nos Aires the holds were cleaned; the tramp loaded grain for Rot-
terdam.

Seven days at sea on northbound passage, Harold Fiddle, the car-
penter (Chips, as he would have been called), decided, after all, that
the milky tincture, the burning flux, was indeed gonorrhea, certainly
not the strain he first had thought it to be. Fiddle, who was no longer
young, viewed the affliction with a serenity that had come with age.

"And how many times is it now?" said Mr. Rowe, who doubled
as ship's surgeon. He injected penicillin into Fiddle's smooth white
buttock.

A methodical man, the carpenter considered his forty years in
ships. He straightened the fingers of his right hand from a callused
fist.

"I believe it is four."

"You're a fool, you know," said the mate.

"It is only a slight indisposition," said the carpenter.

"I'm sure," the mate said with distaste.

The ship moved into the heat of the Equator and under the sun's
solace and penicillin's properties, Fiddle's clap dried splendidly. But
the sun was soon a memory. Achilles climbed the parallels of lati-
tude like rungs on a ladder: into the cold of the North Atlantic and
a rising sea. Behind the sea lurked the wind. And with it came a
lashing rain. The wind, now easterly, increased to gale force. The
gray sea, confused and steep, smote Achilles on her starboard side.
The ship rolled away sharply.

The gale blew for two days. On the morning of the second day,
Carpenter Fiddle heard the sound of metal parting: the amplified

*ping of a blacksmith's plover. Fiddle, who had been repairing a door,
put down his tools. He listened thoughtfully. It had been an un-
usual sound: forward a bit; yes, forward; below the main deck; yes,
somewhere below. Number Three hold? Perhaps, perhaps. He could
not be certain. But soon the hull creaked and groaned again in nor-
mal cadence. All well, the carpenter sighed. No more bangs and
bongs from the deep. Still, he was uneasy. A ship was a flexible steel
box—it would, he knew, bend by design to the pressure and buffeting of ocean waves. Yet Fiddle also understood the limits of torque
and stress. And like most seamen of his day he remembered the old
Anglo-Australian, lost with all hands not far from where Achilles
now labored: split keel to deck in heavy weather like a gutted pig, or
so the board of inquiry had said.*

*Apologetically, the carpenter reported to Mr. Rowe, who in turn
had a word with Captain Tyrrel.*

*"Fiddle heard—he thinks he heard—something adrift below.
Number Three, he says. I'll go down for a look."*

"Take Chips with you," the master said. "And McCabe."

*The mate in company with the carpenter and chief engineer made
his way out onto the weather deck forward of the house. Heaving an
access hatch open against the wind, the three men descended a ladder into Number Three. They played their torches over transverse
bulkheads, the underside of the main-deck plating. Nothing amiss.
In a well of quiet they could hear the muffled booming of wind on
deck. The cargo was all secure.*

It cannot be anything, thought the mate.

*Damned fool of a carpenter! the chief engineer said testily to him-
self—he had been summarily awakened from his pre-lunch nap.*

Abashed, the carpenter clambered out of the hatch. Imagination playing tricks, he ruminated.

On December 18 Achilles docked in the River Maas to discharge her wheat. From there she set out in ballast for the coal tips again at Barry. She had a tear in her main-deck underplating at the after end of Number Three, starboard side. The fissure was of hairline breadth: no more. Invisible to the eye, it ran five or six feet athwart along the edge of a transverse beam. For the moment, at least, it was a minor wound. It had caused little important structural damage. Yet make no mistake: something had happened to the vessel. She resented all that pounding. Wind and sea on the starboard hand: not to her liking at all. In the volatile, oblique, even sullen, way a ship often has, she had tried to tell the carpenter. But Fiddle only wondered what it was that he had heard.

3

December. Brown leaves blew in gusts along the streets. Pale sun filtered through luminous clouds. The air was mild. The air was pale and languorous, yet it seemed to Driscoll that it smelled of snow. Instead, the dry wind blew fitfully and the leaves scraped along the streets like crusts of stale bread. They crushed to dust underfoot.

Late one afternoon, Driscoll and Isabel drove to a boat harbor at the edge of the city and stood at a railing above the water. In the last of the light, catspaws fanned here and there. The moorings held only a few yachts. One, quite near, had a long black hull.

"Will they be taken out?" Isabel asked.

"Probably not. There's no danger of ice. Water is good for a wooden boat."

"The black one is lovely. What do you call it?"

"Yawl."

"Yawl? What a curious word!"

"Do you see the after mast? Look how short it is; shorter than the for'ard one, and abaft the tiller."

"Yes, I see."

"Yawl," he said. "Yawl rig."

She looked intently at the boat. "Could you sail across the ocean in something that size?"

"If you had the stomach for it," he said.

The catspaws fused, a breeze rose, and it became cold. Putting his arm round her shoulders he drew her against his side, the side away from the wind.

"Are you cold?" he said.

"No. I'm fine."

"Are you sure?"

"Yes." Then after a pause. "Let's buy one."

"Buy what?" he said.

"A yawl."

"A yawl? Why?"

"Why not?" she said. "We could sail to the Azores. I know you could find the way."

"It would not be easy," he said.

She did not seem to be listening. "I'm sure we could do it," she mused aloud. "And we could go on to Mallorca."

"We would bore each other," he said.

"No," she said. "We would love each other. We would love each other, Johnny, until we were one and the same person. That way we would not bore each other."

Driscoll gazed out over the harbor without speaking and Isabel, who sensed his restlessness, said: "Are you going back?"

For a time he did not respond. Then taking up her game: "Where do we go from Mallorca?"

"Naples," she said. "Naples, of course. We'll hire a car and driver and go through the city and up the hill, to Vomero. Do you remember how hot it was?"

"Yes," he said.

"The view was immense. Oh, Johnny, do you remember? We could see Ischia and Capri and we could see Vesuvius on the other side of the bay and the boats off Pozzuoli. Then we drove back through the city to the road along the bay."

He remembered all of it now. He remembered the driver turning off the ignition and shifting into neutral on the downgrades to save fuel. It had been a windy day. The wind blew dust from the road into the car. Isabel and Driscoll were coated with dust.

"We stopped for lunch at Torre Annunziata," Isabel said. "You ate spaghetti and cold veal and drank at least a liter of wine, more than was good for you. Do you remember?"

"Yes," he said. "In that heat it is always a mistake."

"I wanted to go on to Sorrento. I wanted to do that. We could have dined on the corniche. But we went to Pompeii. You were obsessed by ruin. . . ."

She turned abruptly toward him.

"I want you to stay."

There is no warning of a landfall on the northwest coast of Africa....
A city, white and gleaming, grew large in the sun.

Part Two

January—February 1950

*T*here is no warning of a landfall on the northwest coast of Africa. Sea joins sky at the darker line of the horizon. Then suddenly, as in a conjurer's trick, the land emerges: a faint blur at the edge of the sea.

Carrying Barry coal, Achilles came in sight of the land in the early morning of New Year's Day. A city, white and gleaming, grew large in the sun. The sky was cloudless, a dome of violet. And beyond the city the desert had brushed upon the earth a pale, elusive wash of copper tan.

"Casablanca," the carpenter said to a spellbound Joe Corcum.

"Belly dancers, Chips?"

"Only in your dreams, lad."

Achilles *discharged her coal and lay empty along the quay. There was no employ, no other cargo. In London old Shawcross tallied the debit of stores and wages for an idle crew. He would not reconcile himself to loss. He bullied the brokers of Moroccan cement, lead ore, phosphate rock. He must have a cargo; he would not be refused. But nothing could be found.*

Shawcross would delay no longer. He ordered Achilles *home in ballast. It was the tramp's first long passage without revenue freight and Captain Tyrrel prayed that it would be her last. He did not want to lose her. Commands were thin on the ground. A fine ship, she was. A capital ship! Breaking in nicely.*

At voyage end, nosing up London River, she rounded the Isle of Dogs—the three long reaches of Blackwall, Greenwich and Limehouse—and into The Pool above Rotherhithe, laying up in Shadwell Basin, on the north bank. Shawcross paid off the crew, offering recall if trade should warrant. A despondent Captain Tyrrel sent his things ashore to Bishop's Park. Young Joe Corcum, hefting his seabag, trudged up Milk Yard to his mum's, in Wapping Wall. Carpenter Fiddle traveled by train to Merseyside; Mr. Rowe to Southampton and then by Solent ferry to Cowes, on the Isle of Wight, where he had a wife and small daughter. But the mate, pleased as he was for a spell ashore, knew in his heart (with a touch of regret, for he loved his home, his family) that he must put in his time at sea to achieve the prize of command.

As he walked down the gangway a man glared up at him: it was Mr. McCabe. Like the mate, the chief engineer, too, felt the pull of the land. McCabe was making for Edinburgh, where he kept bachelor's digs in one of the old wynds off Canongate. But the engineer, bleary eyed and arthritic and sensing in himself, at sixty-three, a profound weariness, sighed deeply and turned over in his mind a disquieting thought. An audacious thought. He had had enough. He would leave the sea. For good. Not just yet, of course. . . .

"A trip or two more, Mister Mate," he confided to the passing officer. "Aye. Just so. Pack it in. What's the good of it? A dog's life."

Nonplussed, the mate walked on.

Late in January, Shawcross recalled the crew, or at least those he could find. Men who had shipped elsewhere were soon replaced, and among the newcomers arrived a thin, tall Dublin youth, studious-looking behind thick glasses—Coffey by name—making his fifth voyage under license as a wireless operator, transferred out of Amphion, *discharging sugar a berth away. With Sparks now aboard—and Coffey was indispensable, for the ship could not sail without him—*Achilles *dropped down London River in ballast, bound for Narvik. There, at the end of the month, she began to receive a nine-thousand-ton cargo of iron ore, for Mobile, in the Gulf of Mexico.*

4

Each day he searched the shipping columns. At last he was rewarded. On January 11 an item found his eye. When he saw it he knew he would not remain. Isabel would not keep him.

The *City of Tampa* was reported by wireless inbound from Southampton, for Staten Island. Instantly for Driscoll there was a tracing of memory: the great city on the Bosporus and Isabel reeling at the head of the accommodation ladder; he catching her about the arm and waist. Confound the woman! Old Smathers would find a place for him. Surely he would do that! Once, the marine superintendent had opened the possibility of command in the line, but Driscoll had not stayed. He had left the *Tampa*; left the company's employ. He had been an ass to leave. Now he would look at the ship again. It would please him to see her. And from Staten Island he would recross the harbor to a maritime canyon of dressed stone: the office of the line, on Bowling Green. There he would put it to the old codger: the *Tampa*, if a billet was to be had. But any ship would do. This time he would stay. The shore had no importance. The shore for him was insubstantial as fog.

It was early morning and he could see his breath.

The newspaper folded under his arm, he stood out of the wind on the after deck of the Staten Island ferry. Rocking in the chop across the bay from the Battery to the terminal at St. George. Manhattan receding. Skyscrapers dusted by snow squalls; now obliterated by curtains of snow. Shafts of sunlight pierced the clouds, flashing from molten water. The ferry slowed, reversed, bumped the pilings. Ashore, Driscoll walked south along the piers. Soon he could see the *Tampa*'s gold funnel; her fine black bows and curving sheer. Her bridge and midship house gleamed like bone in the hard light.

At the head of the pier he went into a bar. It was an old-time bar with a brass foot rail and sawdust on the floor. An upright piano stood against one wall. For the most part, men who worked the docks drank here; and at night there would be sailors and ships' engineers.

A couple of longshoremen sat on wooden stools. They drank beer. They were clean shaven and had clear eyes. They wore heavy coats and corduroy trousers, and their baling hooks encircled their necks, ice-pick points grazing an ear. The only other patron was an old man reading a newspaper spread flat in front of him, a coffee cup at his elbow. Driscoll started: he knew that face.

The marine superintendent was a small man in a dark blue overcoat and gray fedora. The coat hung loose on a thin frame. A cigarette burned between fingertips, the ash flecking the dark wood of the bar.

Driscoll went up to him.

"Donkeys' years, John."

"It's good to see you, captain."

Names and faces paraded before the old man. He connected them to ships. "I sent you second in *Tampa*. A good berth. You were doing well. I had my eye on you. Where did you make for?"

"Farrell Line. Second in the *Endeavor*. I wanted the run."

The marine superintendent nodded sagely. "Cape Town, Durban, Lourenço Marques. I know that coast. Sixty days out and back. A first-rate service."

"I'd had my fill of winter."

"Winter?" The marine superintendent laughed harshly. "Winter's our trade, John. I won't deny it. A trip or two down the Med in summer, mister, but winter North Atlantic. That's where the money is. Our ships live for winter. Strong stuff. In-structive. A school for seamen."

He paused, reflecting. "I would have had you sailing mate by now. You can't jump from line to line. Not if you want to get on."

Driscoll did not reply. His past was intelligible enough. He tapped his newspaper. "Old times' sake."

"She's a beauty, isn't she? A noble vessel."

"I was going to call on you. Have a talk."

"And?"

"There's no work."

The marine superintendent inspected his companion with dubious eyes. "You didn't stay with Farrell, did you? Restless. Adrift. A contradiction in terms. Seafaring is like a ship. Needs stability. Give it up, John."

"No."

"No? Why no? Did you marry? Is that what this is about? In the front door, out the back? Beware, John. We are men of the cloth. Priests in blue serge. The happy sailor has no truck with women."

"There are no happy sailors." Driscoll said. He spoke with derision. "And this is about me: not a woman. The *Tampa* was a good ship. I should not have left." He shook his head. "All of it true," he muttered. "I wanted to tell you. . . ."

Smathers leaned close. His mouth compressed in a thin smile. "I was a happy sailor," he said.

It startled Driscoll to see how blue the marine superintendent's eyes were in the dry brown webbing of his face. It was a shrewd and spartan face.

Smathers pursed his lips, as if satisfied by something Driscoll had said. "I have a place open." He spoke without hurry or particular emphasis. But his tone suggested a clear decision. "*Tampa*. Fourth mate drunk on watch. I've put him on the street."

Now his face reddened. "Christ's teeth! I will not tolerate it! Not at sea. Do what you want ashore, but not at sea. A menace at sea."

He lifted his coffee cup. His hand shook slightly.

"Master and mate won't keep him. And why should they? The sea is not social work. Redemption's not their line of business."

The marine superintendent fell silent. Then he roused himself. "War's in the offing. Should give us a boost—a shot in the arm. We've laid down two more hulls." And gruffly, yet with kindness, for he liked this sailor. "Job's yours if you want it."

"Of course I want it."

"Good. Stop at the office. Papers to sign. You'll join tomorrow. We shift her back to North River day after. You sail Saturday. Master's name is Bride. A fine seaman, none better. The mate, Van Tyne—dickey heart. That's a worry. Skips a beat now and then but the quack is there to thump his ribs. Second's name is King. Ambitious. I'll move him to mate when Van Tyne pulls his pension. The third, Simpson . . . he's getting on. Three, four more trips and he'll swallow the anchor. There's room for you to climb."

Smathers frowned: "One more thing. Don't jump to another line. Don't do that to me again. That's not the game to play. There's nothing in it for you."

The marine superintendent rose to go.

5

She could tell by looking at him.

"You're going back."

"The *Tampa* is at Staten Island."

"You've fixed it, haven't you?"

"I've signed as fourth."

"Don't be a fool!"

"Thirty days, Isabel."

Her voice, strident: "I won't have you here. Not like this. Not any more."

Driscoll had to free himself. He had to do it now. He was free of her. Of the two of them, she was the older. He himself would not age. He was a crafty fellow. He would not decay, as surely she must. He would be an avoider of death.

6

He was aboard by noon. It was familiar to him: the marsh-gas stench of bunkering fuel; white-jacketed stewards scurrying noisily in the alleyways; the rumbling below of engine-room machinery. His cabin, boat-deck starboard side, gave him the comforting assurance of recollected order, solitude and simplicity. His living arrangements were the essentials of a railed mahogany bunk, a maple desk and chair, a green morocco settee.

The chief officer's quarters lay abaft his own, with a view of the well deck aft. Forward were rooms occupied by the third and second mates. The master had his office and stateroom at the head of the file (looking out on the ship's destiny: in port a clutter of hoisted cargo booms; at sea a monotonous vista of spindrift and plunging bows); while the chief engineer—that heat-blanched suzerain of a vast interior space of fire room, boilers, high- and low-pressure turbines—claimed identical quarters, or nearly so, in wary proximity to port, with his assistants trailing in rank astern.

Driscoll's door was ajar. A tall young man knocked briskly, flung up the restraining hook and stepped over the sill. He had fine blond hair receding well back from his forehead. He had high color and a magnificent sandy mustache. His gaze was direct. He held out a hand. Here was a man one could rely on, and also like.

"Dick King," he said. "The mate's ashore with the old man. Anything you need? Help with your gear?"

Driscoll made a sign toward his dunnage and sextant box.

"Whatever you can carry," Dick King said. "Nothing else?"

"Excess baggage . . . ."

"Like a wife."

"Smathers," Driscoll said.

"That's his tune. Still, give the man his due. Something to what he says. We've all had a try. Doesn't last. Not in this trade. Too much to expect."

There was a girl, though, he ventured. On the other side: Bremen.

"Let's get some lunch," the second mate said. "I've scheduled a drill for three: emergency boat, Number One. My command.

You're on the manifest as second. We'll motor about the slip, give you the feel of it. Then shut down the plant and work the oarsmen."

He stepped back into the passageway. "Look here. What about a drink ashore tonight?"

"Yes, I would like that."

A cold wind blew up from the bay, carrying with it gossamer wisps of snow. The two men, tasting the snow, chilled by the wind, drew their collars more tightly about their necks. As they walked from the ship to St. George, Driscoll could see the lights of ferries pushing across the bay in the snow. Then the lights dimmed, and were extinguished altogether. Foghorns and ships' whistles made a desolate sound in the bay. An unseen hand gripped Driscoll's chest. The stirrings of remorse. He could feel, again, his bags pulling at his arms. Isabel had followed him to the street. Her eyes had glittered. He kissed her quickly. There was a taxi at the curb. "Remember me!" she cried after him. "Remember me!"

7

January 14. A darkening sky. A cold, rising wind, presaging more to come. It fluttered pennants on the *S.S. City of Tampa* at her Manhattan berth. The single-screw steamer, thirteen-thousand tons, would sail at four in the afternoon.

Aboard were fifty-seven passengers, the European mails, a freight of meat and other perishables for Le Havre and farm machinery for Rotterdam. Stowed in the 'tween-decks were baled gunny sacks and Singer sewing machines for Bremerhaven. The vessel numbered among her crew the usual complement of officers and engineers, cooks and stewards; and for the special cosseting of her passengers, a ladies' hairdresser and two Filipino bartenders. All said, the *Tampa* was a well staffed and efficient liner: a dependable money-maker for her owners, the Western Ocean Steam Navigation Company.

The harbor pilot dozed in a spare cabin abaft the wheelhouse. He would be called at half-past three. In the chartroom, across the passageway, stood Captain Bride: a powerfully built man; short, stocky, with heavy jaw and brows. He had hair the color of cigarette ash. A scarred left cheek, flayed lip to ear in his youth by a parting cargo wire, accentuated the set of his mouth. His attire was negligent, an idiosyncratic emblem of command. He wore faded khakis, a baseball cap, an aviator's brown leather jacket. The marine superintendent had cajoled, remonstrated. But the master would have none of it. In his own ship Captain Bride would not be dictated to in the matter of dress. Peacock's regalia of gold and blue. Nonsense! he scoffed.

The master raised his eyes. Around him lay the true artifacts of his profession: gimballed and gleaming brass chronometers encased in coffered padding (a pair of reliable Hamiltons, a splendid Ulysse Nardin); boxed sextants wedged securely against the ship's inevitable motion; here a rack of dividers and parallel rules, there a shelf of pilot books; and wide, shallow drawers of charts.

This, then, with the wheelhouse and exposed wings of the bridge was for the master a sanctuary of sorts: not of the world. At sea he would stray below to his cabin for a few hours' repose or a hasty meal taken in solitude. And there would be that occasional graceless appearance in passenger country—the Captain's Table otherwise presided over (rather handsomely, in fact) by the garrulous Mr. Van Tyne or by the young ship's surgeon—his name was Blum—whose charm and mordant wit captivated the blue-rinsed old darlings of the line's Atlantic service.

On the table in front of him the master spread a chart of sea approaches to New York Harbor. Somewhere atop Cholera Bank he placed a weather chit. Winds fresh to strong southwest, shifting west to northwest; temperature falling. The usual storm track east of Montauk. And in the glim of winter light, inbound ships and trawlers would be making for the shelter of Ambrose Channel and the anchorage off Fort Wadsworth. Good holding ground. Safe from the blow. But the *Tampa*, outward bound with the mails, would steam into whatever was brewing: she had a schedule to keep. And so with perverse satisfaction the master scanned the forecast, which told him nothing he had not already gleaned from the cast of the sky and the smell of the wind. Not for him an idler's sleep. In the proper and necessary tradition of his calling, he would be required on the bridge for all or most of the coming night.

It was colder still. On deck, the bosun's gang had battened the last of the five hatches and lowered the cargo booms onto their cradles. Feathers of steam rose from the *Tampa*'s funnel. Towboats ranged alongside, coughing impatiently. Their blunt bows, bearded with rope, nudged the ship.

Mr. Van Tyne—in charge of casting off forward—stamped his feet on a wooden grating. The bosun and the bosun's men huddled nearby. On the docking platform aft, Dick King, tall and straight and resplendently attired in a greatcoat of brass-bound blue, stood outlined against the tenebrous sky. Captain Bride and the harbor pilot peered down from the starboard bridge wing. A few steps away, Simpson, the third, rested a gloved hand on the engine telegraph, while Driscoll, at the wheelhouse door, noted the time in the telegraph bell-book. A quartermaster waited at the wheel.

A crane picked up the gangway, swung it clear of the ship. The steam whistle sounded. Ashore, a flutter of handkerchiefs.

"Cast off the stern line. . . ."

"All clear in the river, Cap. . . ."

"All right, slow astern. . . ."

"Half ahead. . . ."

In the bay and free of her towboats the *Tampa* shuddered as she gathered speed. Fort Wadsworth's green flasher stabbed through the gloom. At the channel's seaward end a lightship beacon silvered the sea. The liner slowed, saw the pilot into a bobbing launch, then resumed her way.

South of Montauk and still on soundings the *Tampa* rolled and pitched like a hobbyhorse through a quartering sea. Ashen dawn crept up over a waste of water. The sky, full of buffeting wind and streamers of dark cloud, was as gray and bleak as the ocean beneath it.

*F*ebruary. *Above the eastern seaboard of the United States cold air from the Arctic burrowed in a long thin wedge below a mass of air that was warm and had flowed from the south.*

Forced upward in a swirling funnel, or column, the warm air rose faster and faster, sucking toward its vacuous center an anti-clockwise rush of wind. As barometric pressure fell, the wind inten-sified to gale force. It pushed up a short steep sea.

After a time the system of boisterous air detached itself from the coast and ran northeast. Deflected by the earth's rotation, it merged with the prevailing westerlies; and on the storm's leading edge a band of wind swept in a two-hundred-mile arc toward lower Greenland. Along the wind's path the sky clouded and darkened. The sea was black. The sea was streaked with foam as the wind shoved it alee. And the wind, gaining strength, flattened the tops of the seas; but some waves fought clear, rising to prodigious heights—thirty feet or more. As the wind steadied, the seas became more orderly.

In the mid-ocean deeps the valleys between the high seas widened. Soon three vast rollers hunched their glistening backs higher than any others. Wind trapped in the troughs molded the water like a blunt hand on potter's clay; extruded the steep-sided rollers into vertical escarpments. The three walls of water dwarfed the dark sea. Under the hard press of wind they raced northeast and east and then south of east across the sea.

On February 4, a clear, cold day, Achilles took departure from Narvik and pointed her bow south along the Norwegian coast. She was down to her marks with ore. She bore the heaviest concentration—some three-thousand metric tons—in Number Three lower hold, with lesser amounts distributed between Two, Four and Five. She carried some of the cargo in the 'tween-decks. Number One hold was empty.

Achilles dipped gently into a flat sea. Her bow nodded, with water gurgling pleasantly under the forefoot, then rose slowly as though awakened from sleep. There was little to disturb the ship's equanimity, or, for that matter, the master's. Comfortably wrapped in a down parka, his pipe drawing well, Captain Tyrrel roamed the bridge, hands clasped behind his back. He could feel the cold against his cheeks. He could hear the wash of the sea, susurrant, along the hull. Here, at least, all was calm. Far to the west a storm had been reported by wireless, with the wind at sixty knots (force eleven on *the Beaufort scale). Close on hurricane strength, the master mused. A thumping blow.*

On the Admiralty's chart of the Western Ocean, Captain Tyrrel had plotted the gale's track from Newfoundland to Cape Farewell, Greenland's southern promontory: and he had drawn a broken line tracing its predicted path east to the Hebrides. His own estimated position on the eighth day of the month, when the storm was most likely to come ashore, would put him five hundred miles to the south, in the steamer lanes west of Cape Clear.

At the mouth of Vestfjorden, Captain Tyrrel stood for a minute or two at the port rail. He regarded the sea. Then—as if recollecting a forgotten task—he stepped briskly into the wheelhouse. He called out a compass heading. He shaped a course to pass between Faeroe and Shetland. The helmsman repeated the command. He eased the wheel. The tramp's head fell off.

Satisfied, the master strolled back to the open bridge, this time to the starboard wing. Abeam, Vaerøy Island jutted from the sea like a shattered tooth. Ahead the horizon lay empty. No drama there. The ocean suggested nothing so much as pewter plate. It was without portent.

Mr. Rowe clambered up the bridge ladder. He, too, glanced at the unedifying water.

"Greenland in for a bit of a dusting," the mate remarked.

"I dare say," the master responded. "Nothing to do with us."

8

February 2. He sat in a café drinking cognac. The café was on a street that had not been damaged in the war. It had paneled walls and a frosted-glass door. Cigarette smoke rose to blackened beams. The proprietor shook hands with patrons as they came in from the street and the patrons went from table to table shaking hands with one another. Most of them were pink cheeked and full of good cheer. *"Guten abend,"* they said. A blind man played a melodeon. Some of the patrons got up to dance, stamping their feet until their faces were red with exertion and their brows damp. From time to time the blind musician put down his instrument: he placed the tip of a finger over the flame of a match and guided the flame to his cigarette.

Driscoll cursed himself for a fool. A pulse had lodged behind his eyes. The girl cradled the back of his head. *"Trink das,"* she murmured, raising a cup of coffee to his lips. Threadbare night-dress: disordered, askew. A child's face in repose. He drank some of the coffee, then lowered himself onto the bed. His head hurt badly now. He needed air. He must have air. It would be a fine thing to walk in the cold to his ship, at Columbus Quay. He left some crumpled bills and went out into the night.

9

They came down on the train across the flat, frozen country south of Bremerhaven. The land, dark and loamy in summer, was hard and rutted now. Men and women in loden walked arm-in-arm in the windy lanes. Wood smoke blew windily from the chimneys of cottages. Winter's dead grasses rioted in the snowy glades. It was a place out of time: innocent of memory.

The train slowed for a bend and through the window of the carriage a blackened city stretched before them.

Bremen was cold and stained with sooty snow. Driscoll and the second mate skirted crumbling walls, the rounded apse of an abandoned church. Piles of brick and junk obstructed their progress. There was a smell in the streets like the smell of fishing boats after the catch had been hoisted ashore. It was something you might think a clean breeze and the sun would clear away. Still, the smell persisted. It spread through the city even as the hard winter wind blew south from the sea. The wind blew across the farm fields of lower Saxony from Wilhelmshaven and Cuxhaven, on the sea, and across Oldenburg and Bremen to the hills of the Harz.

As sailors almost always did in those days, the two men carried parcels containing Hershey bars and coffee, oranges and cigarettes. They walked south on Sögestrasse past the market square to the maze of crooked alleys where Dick King's girl lived, between Domsheide and the river. She lived in a small concrete house like a bunker with her brother and with a woman who was her friend.

"Stay out of the brother's way," the second mate told Driscoll. "He was shot in the head. Normandy. He doesn't talk. He's a drunk."

"What does he do?"

"Dockwalloper. The girl works for the Brits. She wants to go to the States."

"That's what they all want."

Dick King's eyes mocked him. "You think so? Don't be so sure. They'll build this place up. Give them time. They know what they're about. Arrogant bastards, the lot of them."

They pushed up the snow with their boots.

"The friend is a tough-looking piece of work," Dick King went on. "But she'll be good to you."

The house was warm. The top of a potbellied stove glowed. In front of the stove stood a bucket of coal and a small brass shovel. There was a deep couch, a few chairs, a glass-topped table. The walls were bare. Fissures of old damp ran down the walls.

The girl, called Erika, was fair and thin: nineteen; perhaps that, yet older looking. She smiled without showing her teeth. She had hair as fine as flax. The friend was called Maria. She had a round face and a hard body. The brother was a big man with big arms. He was a man who could take punishment. A white scar puckered his forehead. His mouth formed soundless words. His name was Dieter. He sat on a chair next to the stove. There were some bottles on the table, and a cabinet of glasses and crockery stood against the wall on the other side of the room.

The house had the same fetid odor that permeated the streets of the city.

It started to snow again after dark. Inside the house it was festive. They had been drinking since afternoon. From time to time the women sucked the oranges the sailors had brought. The stove glowed; the room was bright and warm. Erika sat on a stool playing a button accordion. She played waltzes and ballads. Her shoulders swayed to the music. She played *Stardust* and *Lili Marlene*. She played a tango called *Weisst Du Noch?* The sound of the accordion was harsh. It had a curious power. The two men sat listening to the accordion and sometimes Maria and Erika sang along with the melody Erika was playing.

Dieter stared vacantly at his feet. His mouth was agape. Dick King sat on the couch with his head resting against the wall. He had a glass of kümmel in his hand. Maria, next to him, sipped kümmel, too; and next to her sat Driscoll, content with the kümmel and with the warm, bright room.

Driscoll liked the caraway-seed taste of the kümmel. The room was spinning a little. He rested his head on Maria's shoulder. He shut his eyes.

Erika tapped out chords in a scale. She began to sing:

Hein Muck aus Bremerhaven ist allen Mädchen treu

Driscoll lowered his head onto Maria's lap. She stroked his cheek.

In den fernsten Zonen
Wo nur Menschen wohnen . . . .

Driscoll fell down a well. Falling, he could feel Maria's cool hand on his cheek.

Er ist ein Matrose mit 'ner weiten Hose

He opened his eyes and sat up. The room revolved around him. A child's game. A playroom.

die Mädchen sind aus Rand und Band

Maria held out a glass. He drank. Then he rose, flushed from the heat. Walls aslant.

sie sehen Hein Muck von der Waterkant . . . .

In the cold air outside, Driscoll breathed deeply. He stepped forward and the ground struck him in the face. He rolled over in the snow; he could feel the snow on his hot neck. He lay on his back and swept his arms through the snow. He laughed into the powdery snow falling on his upturned face.

He did not wish to move. He was comfortable like this in the snow. But he knew, or could sense, that something was wrong with his head and that his tongue, dry and swollen, could not be dislodged from the roof of his mouth. His mind accosted itself with a parable of death. (At least that is what he thought his mind was doing; he was not really sure.) As he lay with his eyes closed, his tongue choking him, a sea wave curled above his head. It was green and foam-flecked and it fell heavily. It drove him down. He could not breathe. He groped for the surface, but disoriented, struck bottom instead. His hands clutched sand. His mother grasped his hair. The great beach at Nauset.

Driscoll had twisted onto his face in the snow. His finger scraped at an icy crust. He got to his knees. His tongue had loosened. He retched. He stood, feet wide apart. Steady now! Oh do have a care!

He went into the house.

Maria extended a hand, as if to support him.

"Let me be."

"You will take a chill."

"Let me be, I tell you."

"Do you want a drink?"

He said nothing.

"Sweet Jesus!" exclaimed Dick King. "Have a drink!"

"Come," Erika said softly to Dick King. She placed her hand under the second mate's arm. She spoke to him as she would to a child. "Come."

Driscoll lay back on the couch. The woman stood facing him.

"I do not want any babies."

"I will not give you any babies."

"Everything is bad enough."

"I told you."

She switched off the ceiling light. Light from the louvered door of the stove flickered on the wall and on her face. Her features, round and blunt, softened in the rufous glow.

Asleep, he cupped his hand over Isabel's breast.

"Don't shut me out of your life," Isabel said.

"I won't."

"I don't want to lose you."

"You will not lose me."

The woman on the couch said drowsily: "What are you saying?"

He made a long journey back to wakefulness. He knew by the sound that it was Dieter and that Dieter was drunk.

Driscoll's right arm fell to the floor. His fingers found the neck of a bottle, which Dick King had dropped. Maria stirred next to him. She had a blanket over her chest and shoulders. A shadow swayed darker than the room. The woman lifted her head.

"Was machst du?"

The shadow, which was Dieter, fell against a wall. Driscoll placed his left hand on Maria's shoulder and pushed her down. The shadow scraped along the wall. The shadow spread like a stain on the floor.

"Du dreckiges Schwein!" Maria's voice was shrill. "Filthy pig!"

And Maria, crying now, softly crying. Driscoll did not touch her. He released his grip on the bottle. He put a hand under his head and smiled. Then the smile, which was not mirth, became a laugh. Soon he was quiet.

He shivered violently in the cold. The stove was dead. Gray light seeped into the room. He looked at Maria, who averted her face. Dieter lay where he had fallen. He reeked of schnapps.

Driscoll drew the blanket around the girl's neck. He went out into the corridor. Without knocking, he opened the door to Erika's room and approached the bed. He rocked Dick King's shoulder. Erika's head rested on Dick King's chest.

"We're late," Driscoll said.

"All right," Dick King said.

"I'll wait for you outside," Driscoll said.

The air was clear and cold. The cold was like a knife against his cheek. In a short time Dick King stepped out of the house. The sky was becoming light. There were people in the street. They were black against the fresh snow. Driscoll and Dick King started through the broken town to the station.

10

Isabel thought: Why had he been so careless of life? Was it because he so feared death? Johnny perplexed her. He was a strange, moody, damaged creature, absorbed in contemplation of himself. She detested his world: the sea's emptiness and isolation. His father's people had been of that world, a slab of rock in the west of Ireland. A lonely place, battened and blinkered like a ship. Fisherfolk and crofters, Johnny had told her. An O' once had graced the patronymic. It had fallen away in the South Boston of his father's youth. His father had been a schoolmaster. A reliable man, careful with money. But a man wanting in imagination and enterprise. Isabel had seen a yellowing photograph of him: a man with bushy brows and a fine straight nose.

Next to him two boys stood. One, tall and blond; the other in a
cowboy suit, a wary expression on his sallow face. He had
round full lips, unruly hair. That was Johnny. And at Johnny's
left, seated, a young woman stared; hands clasped in her lap,
dark hair sweeping over the left side of her forehead. She wore
a damask jacket. She had high cheekbones, Slavic, a bud-like
mouth, and an oval face with wide-set eyes that were distant,
willful, accusing. She had not lacked for suitors, Johnny had
heard her say. No, indeed! She could have had the pick of them.
Had she not been a woman of the arts? Opera had been her
passion. She played the piano with a sensitive touch. Yet she
had married beneath herself. She had married a dullard. But
what else was a woman to do? A steady sort, James Driscoll.
There was that to think of, wasn't there? And Johnny would
recall the day she had burst into his room, head thrown back.
Johnny standing in front of her; his brother, Brendan, a pace or
two behind. Mechanically she brushed a strand of hair from
one eye. What, now, if she were to leave? The words hovered. For a moment Johnny could not grasp their import. Well,
out with it! she had said. Which of us, which one? Choose! And
Brendan, head hanging: father. Johnny, sullenly: father. Ah,
father, was it? Her voice had filled with scorn. And why father?
But Johnny would not speak. And in school, for a time, he did
not speak at all. His teachers did not know what to make of
him, Johnny told Isabel. Consonants locked in his mouth. A
brooding terror of speech. How he had despised his mother!
And father? He had feared and pitied and loved his father. Dear
father, he had written so long ago in a hand that mimed his

father's indecision, his quivering furies. Dear father . . . and I am your loving son. Johnny's past was a palimpsest of amorphous dread. Father carrying Johnny on his back through the waves. And Johnny so frightened of the water. No, father, please no! But father would not turn back. Once, in the salt marsh at Eastham, water had covered Johnny's head. But he thrashed back to shore. Once, on the great ocean beach, upended in the undertow, he had clawed at the bottom. His mother dragged him from the surf. She shook him contemptuously. Had he no sense at all? Could he not tell up from down? And Johnny would say to Isabel, passing a hand over his eyes: "Lord! Trapped by a roof of sand!"

His pain tantalized Isabel. She had engulfed him with her love. Why could she not hold him? And with Johnny now gone she appealed to Brendan, by letter, for explanation, as if reason held the key to her deliverance from solitude.

Brendan responded:

> *I can only tell you that he was a timorous lad,*
> *afflicted by everything and by everyone around*
> *him. In each one of us, dear Isabel, lies buried the*
> *wounded child. Our childhoods overlapped,*
> *Johnny's and mine, but I am the older. I suppose*
> *that if I hid crying because mother and father*
> *were shouting at one another, then Johnny must*
> *have been hiding somewhere, too. If I was*
> *awakened in the night by the sound of mother's*
> *consuming anger—an anger that knew no*

respite—then Johnny, in the bed next to me,
would have heard it, too. I can still hear it as I
write this to you. I cannot shut it out. Johnny was
quiet and introverted, and he escaped as early as
he could and went as far as he could.

Isabel folded the letter. Istanbul, she thought: Istanbul had been her undoing. Had she not had a premonition—a warning of loss—when, those years ago, she walked with Johnny through that terrible city? He, enraptured by the strange, boisterous streets, by the unmusical tongue; and she in his wake repelled by the dust and the filth, by the frenzied hags in raven's black, by the strutting carpet men bedecked in gold, by the food swilled in oil.

But his youth and dark comeliness had bewitched her: the hollow cheeks, the frowning brow, the sailor's perpetual squint. When he spoke, the backward incline of his head—the reclusive, cautioning distance he put between them. The downcurling upper lip, the husky softness of his voice. The melancholy that dulled his eyes—had she imagined this? He was a man for her to nurture, to heal. He was the touchstone of her vanity. And in Naples and on the dusty drive to Torre Annunziata and Pompeii, and in Leghorn and in the lake country above the Lombard plain, the possibility of a life together had grown large in her mind.

Leghorn had been last stop on the *Tampa*'s homeward passage, to New York. For the better part of a week the ship lay in Cappellini Basin loading freight. Isabel rented a car, and Johnny took a few days' leave. With Isabel driving, they followed the coast to Viareggio and Genoa. They turned north across the hills of the Liguri. The sun was hot. They ate a picnic of cheese and wine. They sat on a stone wall enclosing a vine-planted slope. Below them, old women with brown faces and kerchiefs round their heads scraped at the stony earth. Isabel filled pages of her sketchbook. Beyond Pavia and Milan the road passed along the western shore of Lake Maggiore, and in a town called Baveno they engaged a room in a stuccoed hotel. It was a handsome little place with a trellis of purple bougainvillaea flanking the gate. The dining terrace gave on the water. They ate fish as small as whitebait. They strolled on the promenade. The air was warm, windless. In the northeast above Locarno the peaks had snow in their higher elevations. The last of the sun burnished the crags. The sky darkened; lamplight appeared in the hills; the hotels of the promenade were brightly lighted. There was music in the streets, and on the terraces of the cafés the patrons sipped coffee or wine. Not far from shore rowers trolled for pike. The mountains in the west became indistinct. A church bell tolled. Somewhere behind Baveno a train clattered by.

*N*orth and east of Rockall Bank. It was here that frontrunners of the storm rolled under the tramp's starboard beam. Long hillocks of water advanced from the west. Like an army afoot, they marched across the ocean in serrated ranks.

Captain Tyrrel, clutching the bridge rail for support, gauged the seas and the manner in which his ship fell off in their wake. There was none of the slow, deep sliding when a swell rose under the hull. Achilles was as stiff as she had been on maiden run. She toppled sideways into the troughs, swinging back like a steel spring.

The sky was gray, the horizon notched. There was little wind. Smoke from the funnel trailed astern. Morosely, the captain watched *the swells hump across the sea. His mind wandered. The sums and debits of the ship's lading danced in his head. Ton by ton he could find no fault. A violent surge brought him to his senses: water spouted from the starboard scuppers. Bloody cow! He clung to the rail, deliberately searching for order in the notion of unmoving, unmoveable iron-ore—heavier than coal—weighting the holds. He had shifted his southwesterly course more to the south: away from the blow; away from danger. He consoled himself with the thought that whatever was brewing would pass to the north. He was well out of it. Someone else's problem; not his.*

In any event, his vessel was sound. A lively bounce to her step, to be sure, but plenty of upright return.

Achilles *heaved and lifted to the tumescent sea. She stood four hundred and fifty miles southwest of Ireland when the storm, fed at its center by plummeting surface pressures, began to spread in a wider disturbance. An ocean station vessel, code-name* Charlie, *had halted sector patrol: was hove-to in twenty-foot seas south of the fifty-second parallel. And gale warnings first posted for the Hebridean islands of Lewis and North Uist extended now as far south as the Irish coast from Dingle to Cape Clear.*

On Achilles, *the barometer had fallen below twenty-nine inches. The wind, fitful at first, gained strength, gusting to fifty knots. Captain Tyrrel again altered course, but this time bow-on to the rising westerly sea. He would not chance a beam sea. His ship would roll harder yet in a beam sea. He must have wind and wave ahead. What-*

ever was coming would no longer pass to the north. It hammered his nose. He would plow through as quickly as he could. Take his lumps, swallow the wind. There was nothing else for it. Once on the gale's western rim—why, then he would be in the clear.

Huge crests bore down on his bow. The tramp's head sheered ten, twenty degrees to either side of the course. The master loomed angrily behind the man at the wheel.

"Mind your helm, damn you!" Then softly, his voice barely audible above the rising wind: "Hold her, hold her, lad."

The storm petrels were blown from this part of the sea. A kittiwake twisted and fought against the wind. But the graceful bird, in time exhausted, folded blacktipped wings against its body and tumbled into the sea. The whole gale of winter wind flowed east above the Icelandic deeps. It struck to the west of the Great Sole Bank. It lashed at the carcass of the kittiwake and streamed across a ship adrift.

The tramp had been riding easily enough when a towering cross-sea forced her head off the wind. The helmsman hurled his weight against the wheel, but he could not hold her. The insistent wave rose; rose still—its spectral ridge smothered in lace. The ship, too, reared up. She canted to port. On the back curl of the sea she struggled to right herself: but too late. The cargo started an inexorable slide. Provoked by its own momentum, the ore sought a level and shifted in a rush: a rumbling avalanche of dust and rock.

Achilles listed, scuppers awash. Her rudder heeled at an angle too shallow to bite. Her screw, half out of water, flailed at air. Without steerageway the tramp lay helpless, beam-on to the impetuous seas.

The buoyant rollers lifted her high. Like a vagrant gull the ship flew to the wind-flattened crests, only to pause on the lip of a receding slope and drop again to a cavernous trough.

11

In the open Atlantic south of Cornwall the *City of Tampa's* motion had become more pronounced. A storm was making up in the west and a swell had risen out of the sparkling sea. Trawlers nodded in the shipping lanes. Fishermen waved their sou'westers in fraternal greeting. And on the *Tampa's* bridge, master and mates responded in kind.

In mid-afternoon, squall lines collected on the western horizon. They flowed in opaque curtains from sky to sea, obliterating the sun. The west glowed with a yellow light. Flags and tatters of cloud rode on the wind, the wind hardening; rising to gale force. All that night and the next day the westerly wind chalk-scarred the sea. The vessel flung herself about. And in the enclosed promenade, passengers lay gray faced on deck chairs. But the very young children (and there were a few) pranced and tumbled—oh, what glorious fun!—riding with glee the monster's bucking back.

The liner labored under reduced speed. She pushed into a malevolent sea. The wind in the past twelve hours had gained strength. In the drab light of early morning the wind tore froth from the cresting waves—great mounds of water that seemed to taunt the vessel with their bulk before fading away in tassels of spume. The ship now staggered into the seas. She soared on their roiling ascents. A Niagara swept the weather decks. Spray, carried by the wind, struck in sheets against the bridge. The wind whooshed through the shrouds staying the masts, ripping bits of hardened white-lead and tallow from the wire. The particles carried like bullets out to sea.

Driscoll kept watch from eight until noon. From time to time he glanced at the uninstructive radar or made an entry in the log; but without the sun for sextant observations, he had little to do. He grasped the brass rail below the streaming center window. A wiper fanned a transparent arc. Driscoll pressed his nose against the glass; he stared at the smoke of spray. Behind him he could hear the ticking of the bulkhead clock and the creak of the wooden wheel as the helmsman took and gave spokes to keep the course.

The compass card sputtered in its bowl. The wheelhouse doors rattled in their slides. Wind boomed in the valleys of the sea.

The ship went down, found a hollow, then lifted; driving her bow skyward. Driscoll leaned into the cant of the deck. Sickened by the motion, he fixed his eyes on the anchor windlass: a dim lump of metal obscured by flying spray. He feared the storm. He was awed by its power and size. It made a sham of his being. Was there no escape? Better indeed to give it up. What an odd fellow he was! He straightened from a half crouch and squared his shoulders. His giddiness left him.

The master found his chance, then propelled himself deftly up the tilting deck: the wheelhouse unaccountably dark as morning slid toward noon. He lurched against the radar console. On its ghostly screen the seas were motes of luminous dust. No passing ship would be raised behind that veil. Blasted wind! Surely it must come round northwest and begin to ease. The storm, the master knew, stretched across half an ocean: a vast blanket of spiraling air that flowed eastward as he held to a westerly course. The barometer continued to fall. The eye of the gale lay somewhere ahead and to starboard. The master looked for a rising glass and a change in wind direction to tell him he was clearing the blow's southwest quarter. But he did not think he would be so lucky that day.

He turned to his fourth officer, who was buttoning himself into oilskins to join the lookouts planted on the port wing.

"I'll be in the chartroom. Call me if there's a shift in the wind."

The ship rolled onto her side. The master ran downhill. Driscoll made a dash for the lee door.

Directly abaft, the second operator sat typing in front of a board filled with dials, toggles, black knurled knobs. As the *Tampa* slid into a trough, his upper body fell forward. Breastbone pressed to edge of desk. Chest aching. The operator was a young man. He groaned from discomfort. He pushed himself upright. Daydreaming. A job ashore. At one of the seaboard billets: RCA, Mackay Radio. And when it was dark in winter, house bright. A wife.

A Morse transmission from the transoceanic operator at South Chatham, in Massachusetts, chirped merrily in his ear: "And so ends press. . . ." The radio officer unscrolled a bulletin of news from his typewriter and separated the carbon copies for crew's mess and passenger country.

The room's single port was veined with spray. Six bells struck somewhere forward. The second operator looked at the clock: the hour hand touched eleven. He twirled a knob, shifting frequency. Instantly he picked up scattered signals: QTC—"I have traffic." But nothing for him. At fifteen minutes past the hour the thin, piping notes died to static as wireless rooms became obligatory three-minute listening posts: their antennas seeking calls for help.

At seventeen minutes past the hour a broken impulse vibrated in the operator's ear. It was a strong transmission, close

aboard, without fading. There was no slurring of the telegrapher's key. The hand was firm. No nonsense in that hand. It
was Coffey, of *Achilles*, now spelling out his vessel's name, now
repeating her call sign, GKQL. *Achilles* at latitude 49-54 north,
longitude 22-00 west. "Require immediate assistance. Ships in
vicinity please indicate."

The *Tampa*'s operator switched on his transmitter. Filament
voltage registered. He tapped out his sign, WTXY, acknowl-
edging GKQL. "Wire your trouble, old man."

From Coffey:

"Drifting in high seas, steep list, cargo shifted. Power but no
steerageway. Crew 35. TU—thank you—WTXY and position
please."

And from the *Tampa*:

"Hang on a minute, old man."

The operator reached behind his chair for Lloyd's Register.
Achilles; ah, *Achilles*. Bulk carrier, British flag: five thousand
tons. The operator noted the time in his log. He telephoned the
bridge.

Seven hundred and fifty miles to the east, the telegrapher on
duty at Portishead Radio, at the mouth of the Severn, near
Bristol, copied Coffey's message and the *Tampa*'s response. He
strained his ears to catch faint, distant whispers from a Canadian corvette and the hove-to *Charlie*. Both lay well to the
west. Portishead's operator rebroadcast the distress. His powerful signal could be heard as far as Reykjavik and Dakar;

as far, too, as the big coastal station at South Chatham, WCC; and at WSL, Amagansett, on Long Island; and at WSC, Tuckerton, New Jersey. Now across the Western Ocean operators reprieved from tedium adjusted their receivers but remained silent, save for some oaf in the Bristol Channel who had blundered onto the frequency. Portishead's operator keyed a brusque admonition:

"QRT D-I-S-T-R-E-S-S. . . . Stop sending. Ship in trouble. . . . calling for aid."

12

In an attitude of supplication—hands clasped under chin, elbows spread wide on the chartroom table—Captain Bride examined two circled crosses he had inscribed on the Atlantic's northern sheet. Their import was clear enough. Yet for the second time in as many minutes he adjusted a pair of dividers and bridged the marks. As if seeking a hidden augury, he transferred the instrument once more to the latitude scale.

The master nodded. Useless to probe for deeper meaning. The dividers would tell him nothing more. They spanned almost two degrees of latitude: the reckoning in sea miles was one hundred and twelve. Here was a fact he could have confidence in. He, Bride, was separated from the tramp by an overnight run.

The master was alone in the room. Simpson and young Dick King—both off watch—had gone below. Van Tyne would be fussing with the bosun over eternal rust and grime. Driscoll held the bridge. Momentarily the master's thoughts strayed. Driscoll . . . prudent seaman, meticulous navigator—his strong suit. Master's ticket. He had had his war and kept his own counsel: all to the good. But Bride harbored a doubt. Something he could not put his finger on.

The deck rose. The door banged on its hook. Bride's attention wandered back. He remained motionless with the dividers pricking the edge of the chart and the light from a bulkhead fixture shining on his hands and arms. He thought again about wind and drift, time and distance. And, again, he told himself that his was the closest vessel to *Achilles*. The Canadian corvette and the ocean station ship had radioed acknowledgements. But they were too far out of range. There was no question of Bride's being released.

He ran a hand along his scarred cheek, grimacing (though not from pain). Twice he had reduced speed—had been forced to reduce speed—to mollify the besieging sea and ease his passage. Now he proposed additional delay. His owners abhorred delay. He considered, too, the danger of the enterprise: danger to his ship and to his passengers. But he discarded the idea with a dismissive shake of the head. Shoals and rocks nowhere about. The *Tampa* was a tough old sea horse. Wind and wave would not daunt her.

His duty was plain. But by no twist of truth or sentiment could the master say he was pleased. He was not. If duty was the seaman's badge of honor, in this instance he would wear it grudgingly. As for the passengers, he would inform them on the morrow: at first light.

Bride made his way to the wheelhouse, preoccupied with the task ahead. He addressed the helmsman—Driscoll was on the wing. Slowly, from west to northwest, the ship's head came across the hills and troughs. A giant roller climbed the port bow; hung; detonated on deck. The ship pitched down: a loud complaint rose from her bottom plates. The wind blew with terrible force. It picked up the swirling scud and swept it alee.

The ocean was alive with cresting seas; they ran fast and high out of the west. The ship rolled her rail down hard as the summits catapulted a point or two off the beam. Bride braced himself against the incline. He switched on the desk lamp. On his notepad he composed a message to *Achilles*:

"From *City of Tampa* WTXY 48-40 N 20-02 W proceeding your assistance 6 knots heavy seas westerly. Distance 112. Maintain signal for radio bearings. Do you intend to abandon? Bride master."

He hesitated. An addendum: a bit of cheer. Something on the order of . . . will stand by you as long as we have to; will get you off by boat if we must.

No. Not now. Nonsense, that. Keep clutter to a minimum. Especially the last. Don't be an imbecile. God only knew if he could get them off.

Captain Bride turned off the light. He waited for a rising deck; pulled himself along a handrail to the radio room.

13

Half an hour past noon. The seas were building still. They struck the hull with heavy jolts. Driscoll lay atop his bunk. The skin of his back crawled in folds as he slid with the motion of the ship. Sound assaulted him. Somewhere below, the turbine whined. The ocean was full of distant noise. Wind and sea fused in muted threnody. His cabin tilted and sank, and he stared at pea-green bulkheads: a bilious hue. Porthole emitting a watery light. He regarded his books, fallen in a heap on the shelf above the settee: Commander Dutton on nautical astronomy; Squire Lecky's navigation (a turn-of-the-century curiosity; pages foxed, raveled with damp); and an earnest little volume of interest only to the cloth, Mr. John La Dage's *Stability and Trim for the Ship's Officer.*

He concentrated on his books, the reassuring essence of his books—their exposition of a rational universe. But he could not shut out the tumult of the sea. Bride was making for the English tramp. What then? The *Tampa*'s boat. The infernal boat! The sea would swallow it. A dead man's game. No boat could live in that sea. A vision of the boat had shriveled his spirit; had made him craven: the boat smashing sideways against the hull, fall-blocks flailing. He heard an interior voice—fend off! It quavered.

A familiar image came to him. He clung to it. Isabel resting a gloved hand on his arm.

He imagined for a moment that he was walking with Isabel at his side.

14

The west wind had hardened and the temperature dropped. Snow flurries blew down on the wind.

An immense vault of opaque cloud pressed upon the ocean and in the gloom of the wheelhouse the master gazed at the recalcitrant radar screen. It portrayed an image, a nimbus, of electronic snow reflected from waves. The pinpoints of light dissolved and reformed like scattered beads. The master contemplated the problem of *Achilles*. Once in range, would she not fuse with those beads? Surely it would depend upon how low she lay or how far over she had gone, or indeed if she was afloat.

The master would double the lookout after midnight. *Achilles* will have flares. He left for the chartroom.

The chief mate stood behind the second operator.

"Anything yet?"

"Nothing."

The operator slumped in his chair. Though off watch, he had remained on duty: Coffey's pitch and tempo were by now familiar to him. He adjusted his earphones.

"He's signaling."

The second operator typed: "Putting down oil. We will abandon. . . ." A staccato burst of code followed, undecipherable. Then a lull. Coffey again had gone off the key.

The chief mate reached for the message to convey to the master, but the second operator stayed his hand. Coffey had reopened the frequency.

"In a bad way . . . Tyrrel master."

The second operator, moved now by the faithful Coffey, who, like a trusting child, like the second operator himself, was no more than a conduit of someone else's pitiless rhetoric, sought in the springs of his own humanity a word of solace. He tapped his key:

"Courage."

So the name was Tyrrel, mused Captain Bride. A man enticed—as Bride once had been enticed—by the "untempted life presenting no disquieting problems": a man enveloped in the "great security of the sea." (The master had read his Conrad as a religious construes apostolic testament.) But the sea had played Tyrrel false. It now played Bride false. Conrad himself had recanted those words. There could be no security of the sea. The phrase was a bitter corruption. Tyrrel had become a trafficker in menace. Suddenly the *Tampa's* master, angered, abominated the captain of *Achilles*.

A directional loop antenna had settled on Coffey's delayed signal, and now the master, with Van Tyne and Dick King next to him, ruled a bearing on the chart. It linked—it uncannily confirmed—the circled crosses the master had earlier inscribed.

"We can't miss her," the chief mate said.

"You think not?" the master said. "If she floats."

The mate ignored the riposte. He was unperturbed. "Six in the morning. Call it seven. Of course. . . . "

"Let's get on with this," the master interrupted. He turned from the chart. He faced his chief officer. He ordered a course change for drift. And he would increase engine revolutions.

"We'll see how she takes the pounding. Correct as we go."

Mr. Van Tyne went forward.

The master's anger had dissipated. Tyrrel—whoever Tyrrel might be—was no longer his affair. Tyrrel, the man, did not exist. He had become a metaphor of wretched chance: the antithesis of security. Presently the master said to Dick King, who had remained behind:

"There is no comfort in the sea."

"Sir?"

"I said there is no comfort in the sea. Comfort . . . security. There can be no pretense. . . ."

Dick King looked at his commander in astonishment. Never before had this shipmaster encouraged idle talk.

"I'm not sure I follow. . . ."

"I'm speaking of Conrad."

"Sir?"

"This profession. This thing that we do. 'The beginning an illusion, the disenchantment more swift,' and so on."

"Sir?"

"You have not read Conrad."

"Years ago, perhaps. In school. . . ."

How extraordinary! The master paused. His eyes, which had fixed on Dick King's, fell to the chart. Conversation was pointless. That bland young fellow nettled him. The ruddy cheeks suggested youth, confidence, optimism. The master rejected optimism. It was barren, empty. He shifted his gaze once more to the second mate. He admonished him:

"You're off watch, mister. I want you below. I want you rested. You may have to take the boat."

Both men could feel the lift and surge of the mutinous seas. Somewhere below, doors slammed; crockery smashed. Wood rubbed against wood, creaking loudly. The wind cried in the superstructure: a departing spirit.

Again the master addressed his second officer, whose negligent slouch and questioning glance demanded response: "If I send you down—*if,* mind you!—do you hear?—it will be in daylight. Not before. Not in this sea."

Dick King did not reply.

Damn him! "Listen to me. The tramp will have to fend for herself, and good luck to her. You don't go down before dawn. I will not risk it."

The master lifted the doorhook. He hurried to the wheelhouse.

Despite the master's injunction, Dick King made no move to leave. He was drawn to the chart. Its penciled course lines defined a destiny that until then he had imperfectly understood. King was not an unimaginative man. At the same time, he had reflected hardly at all upon his duty as a merchant officer. It was sufficient for him to carry out his quotidian tasks, to observe the sun and moon in their orbits, to take their measure with his sextant, to pace the bridge: and in passenger country to banter and flirt. He was a skilled seaman. If you discounted a weakness for drink—it inflamed him to truculence—he displayed little of what one would call a vice. The life of the sea, with its refreshing sojourns ashore, was congenial to him. What better life could a man ask for? It made few claims on his intellect, none on his emotions. He had accepted risk when embracing the profession of the sea. But risk was imponderable. The master had spoken of risk. "I will not risk it." Risk. . . . What after all is it that one risks? Fear was foreign to King. Not part of his nature. Mewling nonsense! His ambition, if he could be said to have ambition (and the marine superintendent certainly thought he had), was to command—though if pressed he could not have told you precisely why. For beyond a vague notion of "the thing to do," or of a bit of swagger laced with gold at sleeve and cap, or of presiding expansively over the jolly Captain's Table, the essence of command had eluded him.

Until now, that is. Now there was the matter of the boat.

In a lull, in a pit of quiet air, Dick King could hear the hollow clangor of a loose wire slapping against steel. The lull passed. The wind puffed up and struck like a wall. Somewhere forward a sea avalanched onto the deck.

The sea had the power to smash an open boat to scrap.

King, attentive to the ponderous seas and the wind, became dimly aware that the idea of the boat and the idea of command were conjoined; that command was neither pride nor shallow conceit; that command wore the cloak of a noble enterprise and that his master's refusal to debase heroism was the moral imperative of command. Dick King had welcomed the prospect of taking the boat. And why not? It was a lark, no more. Thus he had demeaned virtue. And the ghost of a profound thought came to him: that the seriousness, the dignity, with which he conducted himself in the boat limned a future stripped of pretense. He was certain of his ability as a boatman. He could be relied upon, he knew, not to funk. But success or failure was not at issue. To confront the terror of the sea required humility. The sea was not a lark. The sea cared not a fig for him, for the boat, for his ship, for the tramp. The sea was insensate. The sea was an atomic bonding, a confluence of molecules. It was formless, inchoate. It was a force beyond all reckoning. And so there flickered in the second mate's mind an awakening of humility: the moral surround of command.

15

Directly he gained the wheelhouse the master thought better of his charge to Dick King. The second mate would rest some other time. The boat had to be got ready. It was King's command: let him see to it while there was light. The ship gyrated under the master's feet. He scrambled back to the chartroom and leaned heavily against the door, still ajar on its hook.

The second mate, his eyes agleam, glanced up from the chart. The master spoke through the gap. "Look to the boat, mister. . . ." A premonition stilled his voice. He frowned, uneasy. It cannot be, he thought.

"Turn out the fourth. I want him with you."

The fourth? What was the old boy taking on about? Drains and boathooks: surely one man was enough. "No need, captain. . . ."

"You say, sir!" the master exploded in rage. "The fourth, sir! The fourth! With you at all times. Your very shadow. . . ."

Dumbfounded, Dick King searched the glim of the passageway. The master had vanished.

Fully clothed, Driscoll lay on his side, knees drawn up, hands clasped between his thighs. He stank of sweat. Dick King bent over him, shook his shoulder gently.

"Lend a hand, Johnny. Number One."

Driscoll stumbled out of his bunk. He put on his boots and bridge jacket, pulled a black woolen cap down over his forehead.

The deck heaved up. Dick King staggered, regained his balance. He vaulted over the high sill, Driscoll at his heels. Forward of the fourth mate's cabin they turned down a narrow passage and through a door. Though starboard was lee, wind sucked down onto the deck, tearing the breath out of their mouths. No good fighting that wind. It aimed powerful blows. They raced before it, tumbling into the recess between the motor whaleboat—Number One—and the pulling boat directly abaft.

The air had filled with driving spray. Water streamed down the deckhouse. It sluiced underfoot. The second mate mouthed a warning: "Hang on!" The ship started up an incline, fell back and rolled sharply to port.

The two men hugged the emergency boat's lashed rudder. They looked out upon a scene of desolation. The tossing mountains cradled deep canyons whose overhanging scarps diminished a sky dense with cloud. The sea was black as night. It was marbled and combed with foam. In the west and north a cloud mass blacker than the sea spread upward from the horizon. The wind in the west piped out of that devilish stew: coursed diagonally over the ship.

Driscoll and Dick King made no move to climb into the boat, where the wind was unopposed. They held to their shelter waiting for a lull. Aft, they could see a man fold his body against the wind. He mimed forward motion. He skated in place on invisible blades. Comical, really—a cabaret turn! A harder gust spun him to the rail. But an instant later the wind dropped, and he ran cursing to join his shipmates in their improvised cuddy. His name was Cole: third assistant engineer.

One by one the three men now hoisted themselves into the boat. As if protecting a gilded reliquary they fell on the engine box—the wind again blowing free. They struggled to slide back the hatch. It moved. Cole dropped to his knees; he fumbled inside. Soon a cloud of smoke puffed out of the box, disappeared on the wind. The engine grumbled, caught: throbbed with an unmuffled beat.

Dick King began an exploratory journey forward over the thwarts. He felt for loose gear as he went along. Boat hooks and emergency oars were lashed in place. The towline rigged from boat to ship was looped handily under the second thwart, toggle made fast.

Driscoll, meantime, crouched in the stern well. He would not follow the second mate; he would be blown into the sea if he tried to rise. He was a mote upon the sea. He was frail, without substance. Only the rushing sea and wind had substance. Driscoll would hold out his hand to Isabel. She would not refuse it. He stared listlessly at the careering waves. . . . Hopeless, hopeless!

In the bows Dick King waved frantically. Driscoll forced himself to move. He relashed a lifejacket that had come adrift and poked about the bilge for bailer, drain plugs, coils of line, blankets.

At a signal from King, Driscoll flattened himself against the top of the gunwale and half fell, half slid down the side of the boat to the deck. Cole shut off the engine, and, with the second mate's help, dragged and shoved the lid onto the box. He and Dick King rolled out of the boat.

The three men weaved and nodded like a strange night flower: then pulled apart.

16

Driscoll's funk had not gone unremarked. Dick King pondered his duty. Setting a twenty-five-foot whaleboat into a running sea needed adroit footwork and nice timing. Blocks and ropes flew unchecked. There was the engineer to think about; there were six oarsmen (collectively the spare engine, so to speak). The boat was a contained universe. It was no place for a cripple.

What to do about Johnny? Simpson, the third, was too old for this bit of work. The bosun would go down in a pinch. But the second mate vacillated. Removing Driscoll. . . . Driscoll would be finished at sea.

King wanted no part of that. In his newfound humility he

looked with compassion upon his second-in-command. Who, after all, was Dick King to judge another? Johnny was a decent sort. A seasoned mariner: an engaging enough companion. He had taken a wrong turn; that was it. These things happened. They were bound to pass. King would set the proper course. Chivvy Johnny along if he had to. Driscoll would come out right in the end.

From the wing of the bridge the master, too, had witnessed the curious scene: King crawling busily about the thwarts and the engineer sunk arm-and-shoulders in his box; but the fourth immobile, inert, a lump of clay—staring like a blasted passenger out to sea. What the hell was the matter with the man? A word with him would clear it up. But Captain Bride shuffled his feet and shook his head. The second mate's boat. Unless Dick King broached the subject, the master would let it lie.

17

The first gong had sounded: close on the dinner hour. Three levels below the bridge the surgeon, Doctor Blum, sat at a gray metal desk just inside the open door of his dispensary. Mr. Van Tyne had telephoned a few minutes earlier. The tramp. An overnight slog northwest, the mate had confided. Blum would be on call, of course.

The surgeon's face was thin, boyish. It had an unfinished look. He was armored in white. He braced his feet against the sloping deck. He listened to the crash and rumble around him. He thought for a moment about the tramp, then let it alone. Time enough for that. Absently, he wondered when the first of the evening's sprains and bruises would appear at his door. For no good reason he could tell, they seemed to collect at this late hour. Doctor Blum long ago had decided that the practice of medicine was a donkey's game. It was time-consuming, messy, ineffectual. His patients ashore had got better or worse according to their lights. Nothing to do with him. No sense to the thing, really. And he, Blum, once dazzled by the healer's art and as quickly disillusioned, had come out to sea, where the trade was all splints and nostrums. The work—the ship—appealed. Indeed, his sad dark eyes roved with inward pleasure over a vision, hours old. At the bar, a young woman—thighs ridged round under tight gray tweed. Blum, entering, taking seat next to her. Beer his tipple, bourbon hers. Money there. No mistake about it. Mouth slack. Fond of her tot. Fetched up in this port or that like any dim sailor, or, for that matter, like the surgeon himself. And so, fleetingly, he had engaged in a bit of chat: the war years, drab, tiresome; he at Harvard. She? Radcliffe. Pity; unnoticed neighbors. The ship had swung down. The woman teetered. Instantly the surgeon's practiced hand steadied her deltoid margin, caressing. The woman smiled into her glass.

Blum swallowed the lees of his beer. He glanced at his watch. He signed both bar chits.

"You're sweet," the woman said. "I'm tired of this. There's a rumor. . . . "

"No rumor. Heroics. We'll be out of it soon; overnight. . . . Drink at eight?"

She regarded him reflectively. "Yes. Why not? Eight."

"I don't know your name."

"Nor yours."

"Ah," said the surgeon, gratified by good fortune.

Now, waiting at his desk for custom, Doctor Blum turned the pages, idly, of a magazine. He looked up. He recognized that officer. Driscoll stood in the doorway.

The fourth mate's eyes were red, the rims redder still. Dark pouches hung from the sockets, and his cheeks, once enlivened by wind and rain, were pallid. His face was hollowed by thin and transparent shadows.

Driscoll's hand touched his brow.

"Migraine?" the doctor said. His tone was perfunctory.

"Yes."

The surgeon rose. He opened a cabinet. He extracted a bottle of aspirin.

"Get a couple of these into you."

Driscoll cupped the tablets in an upturned palm. He shrank back. What now? thought the surgeon. The fourth mate was furtive. There was a word: feral.

Abruptly Blum recollected the sound of men racketing about on deck. An engine had spluttered. He looked at Driscoll with attention.

"The boat," he said.

Driscoll did not respond. Useless to speak. Better not surrender to this man's delving gaze.

"It may not be needed," the surgeon said.

"No. If they're afloat it will be needed."

"You don't know that."

"There is no other way."

"You can't be sure, can you?"

"I am sure."

The fourth mate swayed dizzily. He grasped the door handle. The ship lifted: was suspended weightless on the lip of a crest. She pitched over. In his spine Driscoll could feel the shock as she struck.

Lightheaded, the fourth mate stared at Doctor Blum: stared through him. How odd! Driscoll's mind had contracted to an incandescent point. It existed outside the shell of his body. He was not 'himself' at all. Could such a thing be possible? He could see his form from afar, clutching the thick brass handle for support. He was a blurred image. Perhaps he was dreaming. A crack had appeared in his brittle skin, brittle as pottery. A shard fell to the deck. No good putting it back. He did not think it would hold. He expelled air in shallow gasps—exhalations of despair.

The surgeon, thoroughly alarmed, leapt to assist. But Driscoll waved him off. The fourth mate's mind had fused again with its host: corpus recovered. Still, there was a pain so deep he could not dislodge it. A stone in his chest.

"I have to go."

"Wait. . . ." Doctor Blum hesitated. "I'll have a word with the mate."

"No!" snapped Driscoll.

"But why? Good lord! If you're ill. . . . "

"No, I tell you. It's past. . . ."

The surgeon shook his head in consternation. Driscoll had a queer look. They all were a strange lot, tossing about on this godforsaken sea. And he, Blum, no different from the rest. A loiterer on the road to Tophet.

The fourth mate released his grip on the handle. He left the dispensary.

18

There was no moon and no star. There was no light. There was the glint of nearby foam and the chalk marks of white horses galloping over the sea. The ship rolled and strained and beat her way northwest. Sheets of spray dashed in jewel-like glitter across the running lights: ruby to port, emerald to starboard. There were firefly winks as bits of phosphorescence blew onto the ship in the hard wind. The sound of the sea enclosed the ship in its thunder.

Five minutes before midnight. The ritual of watch change. Deep in the vessel a watertight door opened; heat and noise escaped from the engine fidley. Men in flat black caps and white T-shirts balanced sandwiches on the rims of white coffee

mugs without handles. Descending ladders to the control platform, they slid free hands down rails satiny with atomized oil.
The oil glistened on fittings and valves: on the great steel shaft
connecting turbine to screw.

Here below the waterline there was none of the metronomic
swinging of the topside decks. Firemen, oilers and engineers
bent to their nozzles and gauges, shifted about easily in the slower
and more easy motion. The old watch climbed to the deck. The
last man out turned the dogs of the metal door.

A different kind of calm enveloped the navigating bridge.
Eight bells struck. The men of the new watch—officer, helmsman, lookouts—took their places. There was a stiffness in their
stance; they were, in a way, inapproachable: they were isolated
each in his own space as they peered through outer blackness
for a sign: a light, a flare.

It was early yet. *Achilles*, somewhere in the offing, lay too
distant and too low in the sea to be raised save by radio. It
would be hours still: five, perhaps six, seven—no one was quite
sure. "Course three-sixteen," said the departing helmsman.
"Three-sixteen," chanted the relieving helmsman. He whis-
tled tunelessly as he stepped behind the wheel. Mr. Simpson
rounded on the man. "Stow that!"

The wheelhouse was damp and chill. Simpson rested his
shoulder against a stanchion, his eyes fixed on a glowing compass card. It belonged to the radio directional apparatus—
pointer bearing on a Morse transmission from *Achilles*. The
chief operator fiddled with the controls.

A few feet up the deck, Driscoll, relieved by Simpson and at liberty to leave, kept position at the center window. He stared at the scudding dark. Just as well to stay. He was empty of resolve. And into this void, panic suddenly filled his throat with the taste of bile. His head ached dully. A tremor ran down his legs.

The ship was bellicose. She heeled and plunged. Driscoll grazed a neighboring arm. The arm comforted him. It belonged to Dick King. Excited by the hunt and unable to sleep, the second mate had mounted again to the bridge: he, too, peered into nothingness.

An apparition grew large in the lee door, a blacker shade in the unseen night. The master stepped over the threshold. His broad figure was swathed in dripping oilskins. He sank into his bridge chair. He brushed water from his eyes, shut them, let his arms dangle (a puddle quickly collecting at his feet). There was nothing more to be done. Simpson had the watch. Van Tyne had set up camp in the radio room. Lookouts posted on wing and flying bridge, though precious little could be seen in that stinging spray.

To the master's left were shadows. Dick King. And Driscoll. King, mirror of the captain's younger being. A law unto himself. Damn his impertinence! Could he not be disciplined? But the master smiled secretly. No use remonstrating with Dick. Eager to go down; to take the boat. He would have his wish. And Driscoll? What of Driscoll? The fourth mate confounded him. The fourth lived in some haunted past. An illusion?

Slowly the master drifted into hallucinatory sleep. Men and women appeared, brightly lighted, as if on a stage. They made their entrances. They faded into the wings. Hamburg. Doxies he had known, arrayed in courtly gowns: the plush, discreet sporting houses of the Reeperbahn. Old shipmates. His daughter: dimpled mouth, pointed chin, blouse open at the neck. She smiled at him with childish affection, or budding coquetry. It was much the same thing. There was a bond between them that he did not have and had never had with his wife. Captain Bride and his daughter were great friends. She was of a piece with the workings of his mind. Instinctively she understood the melancholy of the sea. And she was proud that her father was a shipmaster.

The master awoke in sudden confusion. He looked about the wheelhouse, with its soft points of light and the uncertain outlines of men. He loved what pressed in on him in the dark. He loved it now in an almost physical way. Its reality was unbearably strong.

For a moment it seemed to impose a sober order upon the mocking conundrum of a life spent at sea: but he knew in his heart it was not so.

From an unseen horizon combers bore down on the tramp.

Part Three

The Wave

Achilles, far down on her weather beam. She rose and fell to the swelling waves: now cupped in a hollow with a sheltering summit as high as the funnel cap; now askew on a crest with the wind running free. Though broadside to the valleys and quivering peaks, the tramp rolled hardly at all. She lay dead in the water, port side low: the seas held miraculously in check, held from breaking aboard, by oil-filled canvas bags sewn handsomely by Carpenter Fiddle and trailing like fish bobs from lines made fast to the bridge overhang.

The oil drifted to leeward more slowly than the ship. It spread its slick wide to windward, trapping the seas—they moved with a sinuous but feeble grace—under its iridescent skin.

Achilles *had power for light and the radio: also for the pumps, although these were nigh useless. Water had found its way below to Numbers Two and Three through riven tarpaulins and stove hatch boards; it had fouled the bilge suctions with a slurry of ore. The screw, too, was stopped, but by master's order: its thrashing had served only to force the tramp out of the oil.*

It was clear now that nothing on earth would right her; certainly not the starboard deep tanks; and that nothing in the end would save her. The cargo of ore, tumbled to port, could not be brought level by hand. Indeed, the list had steepened—the inclinometer screwed to the wheelhouse centerpost registered an astounding thirty-eight degrees. And there was something more. Master and mate—wedged in the angle formed by the dodger and weather bridge-rail—could see plainly in the last sodden light of day that their ship was down by the head. Though Fiddle had cobbled together new hatch boards from scrap, the water forward had done its work.

Time to leave her, thought Mr. Rowe. High time to do that. But how? In ordinary circumstances, if foundering was ever ordinary, they might have swung out a boat and trusted to luck. But these were not ordinary circumstances, not by a long chalk! A few feet abaft, the port boat lay torn from its davits, a gaping ruin. And high above the bridge wing athwart, the starboard boat had jammed in its unnaturally tilted cradle. "Just as well," the chief mate said to himself. "Safer aboard." But he knew better. Achilles was a dying ship. He appended a silent prayer: Let her float a bit longer, Lord; the American was making for them.

The night was black. Seas and wind crashed and roared. From an unseen horizon combers bore down on the tramp. In the eye of the west a crowning wave found a break in the oil, rose through it, hung motionless as if conserving strength for the blow to come: then toppled onto the bow. Achilles *gave way under the cataract. Her head drove off to leeward, then started again to windward. But with Number One hold empty of cargo, the buoyant forehull, though settling, resisted the sea. It bent like a buckled girder. And the tramp—straining mightily to come back—burst her stitches, as it were: ripping open like a sardine tin at that long dormant tear in her underdeck plating.*

Fiddle heard it: the sharp, flat report of sundering metal—he felt the concussion of it, too, in the soles of his boots. He knew, of course, that the deck had gone. And he knew now, unmistakably, what it was the old girl had been trying to tell him those months ago. Ah, that thump, that bong from below—what an idiot he had been! Too thick to understand. The ship deserved better of him. But belay that! Look after her now. Best get up to the bridge.

Mr. McCabe was of the same mind. He, like Fiddle, had heard the shock; had bolted out of the engine room like a terrified mole. The two of them, Fiddle and McCabe, collided at the fidley door. They clutched each other in the heaving passageway.

"That's done it!" cried the carpenter. "The deck. . . ."

"Aye, man; aye," was the response (the chief engineer knew with as much certitude as the carpenter what that carronade had been). McCabe doubted now that he would get out of it alive. And doubt filled him with longing and despair. Did he not remember? That day on the gangway? A trip or two more, he had said to the mate. Pack it in.

A cosmic joke.

The two men disengaged. With Chips in tow, McCabe clambered up the wheelhouse companionway.

Young Joe Corcum, too, had heard and felt the violent jar, but without any inkling of its source. What possibly could he know about the structural members of ships, the strength of steel? They lay outside his meager experience. Vaguely, he fathomed that whatever had caused that cataclysmic thump foretold peril heaped on present danger. Suddenly he began to sob. His body shook with paroxysms of fear. He could not brazen it out. He did not have the will. Gone were his days of swagger on the Thameside docks. He knelt in a passageway. He clasped his hands under his chin. With tears rolling down his upturned face he called aloud: if this time he was spared—this one time!—he would never set foot in a ship again.

From his post on the port wing, Captain Tyrrel could see nothing of the well deck forward. "Mast lights, quickly!" But Mr. Rowe needed no encouragement. He was by this time halfway up the bridge, scaling the slope as if his life depended on it (which it surely did). He bawled an instruction through the wheelhouse door.

The floodlights came on under fore and mainmast crosstrees. The fore part of the ship gleamed with spray and wind-blown oil. To starboard a few feet forward of the house an inches-wide fissure opened out of the deck: tracing its cleft downhill to port, to the weather scuppers now awash: climbing the bulwarks in a jagged rent—a terrible wound.

"Winch drums, Mr. Rowe!" commanded the master. "The wire! Fore and aft! Unship the wire. Haul it through the alleys. Brace to the bitts. Lively!"

The mate retreated down a ladder aft.

Captain Tyrrel cast a greedy eye forward. Oh for that chain! Breakers swept the bow, inundating the anchor windlass. The master could think of no way to sever the massive couplings, much less work those tons of metal aft. Not with this list. It could not be done. No man could keep his footing on that half-drowned fo'c's'le head. Yet for an uncertain moment Tyrrel was tempted to try. Call for volunteers. They would not fail him: not the sturdy Mr. Rowe. And Chips! And that young bullyboy, Corcum. . . .

Come to your senses! He had no stomach for another man's death. He would do what he could with cargo wire—a cat's cradle strung from drums to bitts. The wire was their only hope. The gift of time.

The chief engineer, coatless, shivering in the cold wind, skittered out of the wheelhouse and along the cant of the wing. He grasped the dodger. He peered down at the deck. The master's mouth was at his ear.

"Wire . . . " the master croaked. The words that followed blew away. McCabe got the drift. Wire to hold the break. And McCabe in his turn looked longingly to the windlass: but he knew as well as the master that the chain would not be moved.

"Power for the winches, Mr. McCabe. Must keep power on . . . at all costs. . . ."

"Aye," shouted the engineer. His voice, stronger than the master's, rose above the wind. "Power you'll have. But look! The port bulwarks!" McCabe thrust out his arm. "Do you not see? She's bound to be taking water in Number Three."

Captain Tyrrel gestured impatiently. Water? Was the man daft? Talk now about water? "The deck, Mr. McCabe! The deck! Will wire hold it?"

"Who can say?" cried the engineer. "She won't stand much more. . . ." *McCabe was no coward. But he cringed from the sea.*

The rollers bulged large under the oil. They lifted the ship high, dropped her back giddily. In the light of the crosstrees the men of Achilles *could be seen doubled under the weight of the heavy cargo runners: toiling forward like oxen in their traces. They balanced as best they could; gained precarious footholds on seams and fittings. They made progress slowly. Each step was a small victory on that slick and treacherous slope.*

Mr. Rowe bellowed an order. He waved his torch. The men dodged clear of the wire.

The winch drums revolved, reeling in slack. The wires came taut across the fractured deck.

Coffey, tormented by his own youth, surprised by how much he wanted to live, by the intensity of his will to live, who did not think he would live until dawn, sought in God's providential plan for him a prescription for right action. Propped on a lifejacket to keep from catapulting from his chair to the deck, the radio operator vowed to look audaciously upon death. Still, his seditious mind confounded resolve. He shook his head in anguish. Now alive. Tomorrow not. Suffocated in this blasted tomb! He shuddered at the savage imagery. In desperation he clung to the notion of faith drummed into him by the Christian Brothers of Synge Street. Magis enim fidelis, *and all* the rest of it. Thomas's postulate of creed. The evidence of reason rebels against faith; yet the believer assents to the truth of faith.

Assent! That was it. He had puzzled over Aquinas but, yes, that was the key. Assent to the truth of faith. What could be simpler? And so for Sparks it remained an elemental truth that God existed. A recognizable God (a bearded ancient: a celestial charioteer). God the comforter: the grantor of life everlasting to those who seek Him.

The door banged open. Coffey felt in the current of air the benign finger of God. The master, hollow eyed, chin stubbled, had thrust a slip of paper into the operator's hand.

Coffey collected his wits. He tapped out a transmission:

"Foredeck split athwart. Bracing with cargo wire. Shipping seas through oil. Make all possible speed. Situation grave. GKQL."

On their hands and knees, master, mate and chief engineer huddled in the lee of Number Three's coaming. They stared at the breach. The opposing edges of metal had begun noisily to shift, to grind like millstones.

The master got to his feet. In vain he scanned the southeast. The American. Bride. In the offing. But where? Time, thought the master. We must have time.

The mate, too, straightened from a crouch. And like the master before him, he fixed his eyes on the tramp's shelterless bow, awash in a torrent. The chain! Yet even his agile mind could see no way of freeing the links. He looked down at Mr. McCabe, who, supine, sighted along the wires bracing the deck. "They will not bear it," said Mr. Rowe. "The strain is too great. The ship is done."

The chief engineer rose. He chortled bitterly; he wagged his head. "I've had this coming," he said to the mate. "Oh, indeed, indeed!"

A parachute flare, then another, and one more, flew from the ship's bridge: dazzling red streaks that dimmed to indistinct radiance as the wind swept them alee.

Abaft the house the bosun and his gang had overhauled the heaviest of the hoisting gear: stripped the jumbo winch of its wire. The men formed a straggling queue. They grunted piteously. They divined the futility of what they were doing. They dragged the wire into the starboard alley. Carpenter Fiddle led the column, the bitter end over his shoulder: a reluctant Joe Corcum—prodded by the swearing bosun—followed a few steps behind. They reached the foredeck, the coaming of Number Three. They were trapped in the crosstree lights, a tableau. A sea suddenly lifted to port: black and towering: implacable as a cliff of tar. A fringe of white lace flapped at its ridge. It was the first of three giant rollers that had come along a curving track across half an ocean.

The sea reared up out of the oil. It overhung the ship. It mounted the port rail.

Fiddle heard the sea as much as saw it. But what he heard was the sound of silence, for the sea had blocked the wind. The foredeck was a well of quiet.

The carpenter cried out. He dropped the wire and scurried eagerly up the deck. He tumbled on top of McCabe and the master. Joe Corcum, crawling behind like a lizard, got his arms in a muscular grip round the chief mate's neck. The mate struggled for breath. One of the boy's legs straddled the rent.

The upstanding sea—impeded by the tramp—curled and col-

lapsed. *Pressed down by solid water, the little ship oscillated like a pendulum, then rode up the flank of a second sea, the first sea gathering its skirts and sailing erectly off to leeward: the second sea welling under the ship, and the ship dropping into a following trough.*

A third sea loomed. It extended laterally, unbroken. It nodded its lofty head, fell hungrily on Number Three—devouring canvas, shattering hatch boards.

The four men and the boy seized whatever they could for support. They gasped in the vaporous smother. The bow twisted: the foredeck sagged. One by one the wires cracked like gunshots. They whipped the spume-filled air. As the sea cascaded into the exposed hold the vessel came apart at the break in the deck.

In no more time than it might take to groan, or to rub an eye in wonder, the after part of Achilles *rolled onto its back: was driven below the surface.*

In Coffey's tomb a word formed on the Dubliner's parted lips, and one suspects what he was trying to say. But he made no sound.

The foredeck had gone black. Mr. Rowe somehow had managed to hold on to his torch. Its beam found the boy. He lay curled in a heap. Blood pulsed from Joe Corcum's left leg: nothing more than a scrap of dungaree, a splinter of bone.

The master squirmed from under the carpenter and chief engineer. He looked aft into darkness. Darkness was where the rest of his ship should have been. He was not sure he understood. The crew. And

Coffey. Coffey at his key! He had left him minutes before. All gone. And why was that boy yelling so?

The fore end of the tramp, buoyed by the empty Number One, raked its bow skyward: a tangle of wire and sundered masts. Joe Corcum's caterwaul subsided to a noisy whimper. As tenderly as they could, Fiddle and Mr. McCabe drew the lad a ways up the incline. They made fast a length of loose rope around the stump of his leg, above the knee.

19

At four in the morning of February 10, this message had come from Coffey: "Make all possible speed. Situation grave."

And from the *City of Tampa*: "Are you firing flares?"

From Coffey: "Do you see us?"

Insistently from the *Tampa*: "You are not on radar. Are you firing flares?"

Coffey: "Affirmative. Do you see us?"

The *Tampa's* lookouts saw nothing.

Coffey again radioed: "We are firing. . . . "

Here the transmission ended. The *City of Tampa* called *Achilles*. Coffey gave no sign he had heard.

"I can't raise her," the second operator said to Mr. Van Tyne, who was serving as bridge messenger.

"Keep trying."

"I think she's gone."

"Send a general call."

The operator tapped his key. "WTXY. Does anyone hear GKQL? We have lost contact."

In the Bristol Channel, Portishead Radio said it had lost contact.

In the west the corvette and *Station Vessel Charlie* and the oceanic wireless posts at Tuckerton and South Chatham had lost contact.

Mr. Van Tyne went to the wheelhouse. He paused in front of the radar console. He was arrested by the enigma of its arcing beam, which offered no enlightenment on twenty-mile range. The deck rose. He cocked his head, expectant. He tightened his grip on the console frame. This would be a big one.

A parade of lofty combers swept at speed out of the west. Two of the whalebacks rolled under the *Tampa*'s hull; a third, high as the bridge, higher yet, curled capriciously, smashed down on the bow and plucked the unmanned lookout's pulpit from its weld: tossing a ton of steel plate over the side—just like that!

The ship sank into the trough. She burrowed her snout deep

in the sea. She came back heavily, as cataracts swept with abandon down the foredeck and spurted alee.

The *City of Tampa* trembled under the blow, but other than the missing lookout's roost (unseen in the dark) and the usual detritus of crystal and crockery, not much damage had been done. There was a good deal of bruising about—nothing serious, thank heaven!—and the good Doctor Blum soon was in bustling attendance. On the bridge, Driscoll and Simpson had rollicked wildly on the starboard gratings, while to port the master and Dick King clung to stanchions. The master marveled at the strength and resilience of his vessel, plowing up vertiginous seas that straddled all of the Western Ocean: seas that would break a lesser ship: that had, he was certain, broken *Achilles*. But there must be no doubt. He pulled himself through the wheelhouse door. He would hold his course another hour at least; then begin a widening box search for wreckage or survivors. But surely no man adrift could outlast this consuming sea. The master felt neither pity nor regret, only lassitude, weary relief; as though he had been excused from an onerous duty.

Instantly abashed, he scolded himself for faintness of heart. He ordered flares fired at ten-minute intervals. The men of *Achilles* would answer with flares of their own if any of them still lived. He returned to the wing.

The *Tampa*'s flares burst high, white flashes of illumination that blossomed like water lilies before being caught up on the wind.

Their pulsing brilliance lit the underbellies of cloud that stretched in a canopy across the sea.

At four-forty a star, or spark, gleamed on the horizon. Captain Bride stiffened. He alone had seen it. He lowered his binoculars, passed a hand over his eyes. *Achilles* risen? Preposterous! Where were her range and running lights? Distress rockets? He resumed his study. Through a cloud rift the star sat low in the northwestern sky. Then it was lost. The master strode into the wheelhouse. The radar was noncommittal. He made his way back to the wing.

Distracted, the master scraped at the rim of salt in front of him. The dodger was coated with it: greasy to the touch. On his brow he could feel the wind and he judged the cresting of the seas by the motion of the ship. There again!—that goading light.

"Broad on the port bow, Mr. King. Do you see it?"

King could see it.

In added corroboration, a lookout on the flying bridge called out the sighting. The distant light blinked on and off. It seemed to hang on a peak, then douse in a hollow. The *Tampa* worried a point or so to port, northwest by west: lured by that drifting ember.

The chief operator, climbing to the flying bridge, worked the signal lamp. Its glare stabbed and stuttered in the dark.

The spark on the horizon made no intelligible response. It beckoned them on.

Captain Bride cursed his unruly radar and that maddening light. Answer, damn you!

He had no way of knowing, of course, that what guttered so oddly out of the night was not some dimmed lamp of a listing *Achilles* but Mr. Rowe's torch: turned on when the tramp's mangled bow soared to a ridge; turned off in the trough to conserve its uncertain glimmer.

20

Astern, in the southeast, one could sense rather than see a faint abating of the dark—a smoke-gray smudge, a thumbprint on the night.

The fugitive gleam that diffused from the gray-breaking dawn illumined a gray and shifting desert. The sea was wind-etched with white. It rolled in billows from the west. Combers crested in crystalline showers of froth.

The *City of Tampa* threw her screw into the air. The screw raced; it fell back to bite again.

Upwind of the liner a black object floated.

The forepart of *Achilles* lay portside down to windward like a monstrous steel raft: prow high: the surrounds of Number

Three hatch a litter of wire, mast stumps, shattered plating. The hulk rolled very little. A sea bore it aloft, then dropped it into a trough.

On the raised side of the foredeck, which was to starboard, five men could be seen in the lee of Number Three's coaming. They pressed their faces to the deck. They took little notice of the looming shape to leeward. Now and then a sea crashed uphill across the wreck. Wind and momentum carried the water alee over the upper bulwarks, but a residue drained downhill like a wide, shallow undertow.

The cold water washed round the men. They did not draw away from its grasp.

As Captain Bride stared through his binoculars, a man on the wreck rolled onto his back. It was a slow movement, full of unconcern; the sort of thing one would do under a shade tree on a summer's day. Yet the man—a boy, really—had but one leg. A rag-end of cloth and a length of line protruded halfway down the other. An older man tugged at the boy's chest: pulled him closer to the sheltering hatch. The older man's arm rested protectively over the boy's shoulders.

Captain Bride lowered his binoculars. He looked now at the clouds. They scudded beneath a dense overcast. The sea was high. The wind keened in the rigging. But the wind had shifted a point to the north and the glass had risen. Bride's sense of the sea told him that a break in the gale would come with the wind shift and barometer gain.

He prowled the port wing, scanning aloft then back to the wreck, which the liner circled like a predator wary of prey.

Soon the *Tampa* halted to windward. Her bow was on the sea. She kept position with engine at dead slow. The master considered the combers that moved with stately gait out of the west, a bit north of west. His body swayed on the tilting deck like a reed sunk in shifting soil.

Eyeing the seas with disapproval, he reckoned the business of putting down a boat. Nothing of importance could be achieved from the ship. Her very size conspired against him. The hull was a sail. In this seaway, with this wind, the liner would not be controlled. The work the master had to do was too fine. The wreck was a half-submerged reef—he dared not move in too close.

Soon there would be a fall in the wind and an easing of the seas. The motor whaleboat would get away smartly from the *Tampa*'s side. Dick King, at the tiller, would fetch up to windward of the wreck, would keep well clear: holding the boat's head to the seas. Get a line aboard with lifebelts made fast. Still, take care! Take good care not to drift down. He would be stove if he so much as touched. King must stand off. . . .

Those fellows on the wreck must know what they had to do: slide down their weather side and into the sea on Dick King's line. Dick would fish them out. One by one. . . .

The master broke off his ruminations. He leaned on the rail. His glance fell again on the boy. This one would not live; he slept the sleep of the dead. The man next to the boy, the older man, now roused himself. He lifted his chin. It was caked with salt. He stared indifferently at the plunging liner. For the first time, he raised a fist in bleak acknowledgement.

Bride withdrew a pace or two up the bridge. What had he overlooked? King would sustain the master's faith in him. A superb seaman, if Bride was any judge. And with the survivors in his bilge, Dick would stand downsea to where he, Bride, would hold with a lee, a shield against the wind.

Mr. Van Tyne stood close by. A moral distance now separated him from the master and he would not intrude. He waited for orders. Dick King and Simpson came up behind. Driscoll hung back in the wheelhouse door.

Dick King alone stepped forward. He defied convention. He would not be contained.

"They won't last. . . ."

"Not yet, mister. Soon. You'll go with a lull."

Bride's voice was harsh above the wind. It rasped. It recalled a secret foreboding. It forestalled a wayward child.

The boy had lost much blood. He lay yet on his back with the wind blowing coldly over him and felt not the cold but a strange debility. He was empty and tired and his left leg was numb. He was engrossed in the gray sky and did not think. He had been afraid, but was not now, and he did not think about death.

"Look there, captain," the chief mate said. He had raised his head level with the hatch coaming, and he peered across the sea.

Captain Tyrrel got to his knees.

"Yes," he said, gazing to windward.

The City of Tampa *rose and fell with the sea. Her bow threw screens of spray. She was scabrous with winter rust and her motor whaleboat seemed small and fragile high above the rolling sea.*

Men could be seen scrambling into the boat. Their orange lifejackets moved to and fro: a display of gorgeous color in that infinite grayness.

For a time now the wind had hauled into the northwest and begun to moderate. But the massive seas, released by the wind, romped freely, falling back upon themselves in a tumult of foam.

With the wind still dropping, the seas began again to form ordered outlines of ranked waves. In time the ranks became clearly delimited crests separated one from the other by quarter-mile hollows.

The seas ranged high. They moved fast. They did not comb as they moved with the wind.

"It's the drink for us," the chief mate said. "The boat will fetch up to windward and it's in we go."

The carpenter and chief engineer were also on their knees, staring across the sea.

"Are you a strong swimmer, Mr. Rowe?" the master said.

"Why, yes, sir."

"Good, then. You'll take the boy."

The mate nodded; he did not speak.

The chief engineer turned to the captain. "Will they float a line?" He was becoming confident as he looked to windward at the men in the boat. He allowed himself now the luxury of hope.

"I should think they'll stand in close; heave one up the hatch,"

Captain Tyrrel said. With a swift glance he took in the steep wet slant of the deck. "It's a long throw. But the wind is right."

"The sea is very high," the chief engineer said doubtfully.

"If they're boatmen they'll come close aboard. Close as they can get without staving."

The wreck soared on the curl of a sea, then fell back, this time rolling hard. The sea poured across the weather bulwarks, forming swirls and eddies. The four men dropped prone; they hugged their bit of deck. The boy groaned a little and pitched over onto his face. Turning him gently, the master pulled the boy against the coaming. The boy had lost consciousness. His face was a sickly hue, beaded with moisture.

"How shall we cross, sir?" the carpenter asked, shivering in the cold.

"We'll go one at a time except for Mr. Rowe and the boy. We're certain to have a stout bit of line made fast to whatever light stuff they heave up to us. Kapok, too, I expect. Each of us will wait his chance down the deck; then over the side—those remaining hauling back slack. Mind you, a good grip on the line, Fiddle, and take a turn round your chest."

"The water will be terrible cold," said the carpenter.

"You won't be in it long, Fiddle," the master said.

"Aye," said the carpenter.

"Let the boatmen pull you over. But use your arms to help them."

"Aye," said the carpenter. He looked at the water with distrust.

"Will you go back to sea, Fiddle?"

The carpenter pondered. "If there's a ship to be had."

"Quite right, Fiddle. Quite right." And the master thought: what of commands? Will there be a ship to command?

The chief engineer arrested the captain's musings. "The boy will not go back."

"No," the captain said. "He cannot go back."

"Ah . . . the poor lad," the carpenter said.

"They'll have a doctor," the chief mate said.

"Fat lot of good it will do!" the chief engineer blurted. "Are you blind? Look at him. He's done for."

The others said nothing. The boy's lips trembled in imitation of life. He lay very still. The wind blew over the wreck and fluttered the bloody rag of trousers below his severed leg.

"He was a good lad," the carpenter said.

"They were all good lads," the chief mate said, glancing astern to where the rest of the ship once had been.

The captain raised his head above the coaming. He, too, peered astern. His perplexity was transparent. Good lads. Decent lads. Young Coffey. . . .

A sudden movement caught his eye. Across the sea the Tampa's whaleboat descended the side, cushioned against the liner's rolling by a long ragged fender of mattresses and cargo nets.

"You'll go first, Fiddle," the captain said, jogging his mind to the discipline of command. "Then you, Mr. Rowe—with the boy. Mr. Mc-Cabe will help you down. Mind you, Mr. Rowe, a French bowline round the lad: keep his chin up as best you can. I'll bring up the rear." He paused. "Good luck, all of you."

"Good luck to you, sir," the chief mate said, his voice loud with emotion.

"We have a very good chance, Mr. Rowe. God bless you."

"And God bless you, sir," the chief mate said.

The captain thought: God bless this ship and all who sailed in her. All those lives gone. And now the boy. And what of himself?

21

The liner slid quartering into the seas, knocking them down and making a broad fanning slick on the starboard hand.

The whaleboat bumped the fender on its way to the sea. Dick King braced his left leg in the steerer's well; his right knee pressed against the starboard bench. He crooked his neck over the side. On deck at the winch brake the bosun lowered the pendant craft. The ocean rose to meet the keel. The lee made by the *City of Tampa* was smooth and wide, but lumpy seas were showing now beneath the ship's counter.

King listened with satisfaction to the beat of the engine. All was as it should be. It rumbled and snored. The third engineer, Mr. Cole, crouched in the bilge, adjusting the throttle. He faced aft. Driscoll, kneeling uncomfortably on the bottom boards, grasped a metal bar, waiting for word from King to pull up on it and free the boat from unspooling falls. Driscoll could see the hulk of *Achilles* and the gray seas rolling under it to leeward, hoisting the wreck on ascendant shoulders, plunging it into enveloping troughs. He looked up. The *Tampa*'s passengers had attached themselves to the starboard rail. A woman raised her hand in tentative salute. The gesture was futile. She caught Driscoll's eye and would comfort him if she could, but she could not. She offered no consolation. He envied her rooted ease, the solidity of the deck she stood on.

Driscoll could see motes of stack soot falling upon his arms like blackened snow: they powdered the back of his gloves, his kapok lifejacket. A manrope dangled temptingly from the davit crosswire. He would climb it. Or the nets. Slung over the mattresses, the ladder of nets. He would climb that ladder; leap into the nets. Yet his limbs were palsied. His hand nudged the releasing lever. "Steady!" bawled Dick King above the engine's guttural.

The boat descended.

King, his knee still pressed to the bench, his left forearm revolving indolently in a signal to the liner's deck, looked down at the slick and a little ahead. He calculated the narrowing breach. Not yet: he had yards to go. His crew gripped the thwarts. A swell surged under the *Tampa*'s counter. It moved to intercept the boat. It mounted suddenly to a greater height. Whether Dick King saw it, no one could later say. "Release!" he called. Driscoll pulled up hard on the bar. The boat's supporting wires and blocks unhooked: an explosive report. The cockleshell's bow declined at an acute angle. The billowing swell cradled the stern, buoyantly lifting, lifting: then flinging the delicate craft clear of the fender in a scrape and clamor against the ship's side. Someone sang out a warning. King looked surprised. He did a curious thing. He extended both of his arms as if rushing to an embrace. It was grotesque. Perhaps he was trying to fend off. But from his position on the starboard bench it was impossible to fend off. Perhaps he sought a flying manrope to steady himself. No matter. He fell backward onto the gunwale. The stern of the boat, rising still, acted as a fulcrum against his arching spine. It levered him into the sea.

"Dick!" Driscoll yelled.

"No use! No use!" cried the bowman.

"Too late!" from Mr. Cole.

"Your helm!" the bowman screamed.

The boat had snubbed its towline and was dragging along the hull. Driscoll fell on the tiller. He gave it a mighty push to port. The boat sheered off from the ship's overhang. Aloft, a confusion of shouts: "The toggle! Pull it! Pull it!" The bowman, who lay sprawled across a thwart, righted himself and found the wooden pin. He yanked it loose. The towline snapped into the air. The bow, released from strain, rose and threw back spray. Cole advanced the throttle. The boat dropped into a trough, then climbed to the crest of a following sea. The whaleboat steadied, hovered momentarily: and

Driscoll, looking back, could see the ship, and it was far away.

On the bridge and at the rail they had seen the second mate go into the sea. They had seen the bright orange of his kapok speed aft along the hull. Captain Bride raged. His hand was on the engine telegraph. But King was lost to sight under the stern before the screw could be stopped.

The master looked out to sea. He searched desperately through binoculars. Four white ring-buoys rose and fell. Hurled from bridge and fantail, they marked the acre of ocean where the second mate had gone in. The whaleboat—downwind—had begun a turn into the sea: turning back to the cluster of buoys. Alee, the wreck of *Achilles* lay dark and small in the sea.

The master lowered his glasses. He knew his second mate had got in the screw and there was no finding him now.

We just let go, Driscoll said to himself, and that was the end of him. He spied a buoy and tatters of orange kapok: rumors of a forfeit life. He could make no sense of it. His mind was racked with disorder. He was beset by shards and scraps of disconnected thought.

Upwind, the *Tampa*'s horn trumpeted its charge. It made a tyrannical din. "Leave off and follow me," it commanded. There was nothing else to be done. Those bobbing eyelets covered a grave. The liner heeled, bowed in farewell, and turned aside. She steamed downsea. She rounded the wreck, but stood clear.

In the lowness of the whaleboat the troughs were cavernous now away from the ship. Driscoll shoved the tiller over and the cockleshell shot off to leeward. There was a delirium of nausea: but his demon had melted into the marbled canyons. His mind had become an empty vessel. He filled it with the steering. He used the wreck as a marker and came across the sea.

22

A great anger compounded for the most part of his own helplessness had welled up in Captain Bride. He was puny and contemptible. He controlled nothing. He was master of nothing. Command was a fiction. He uttered an oath. Dick King had been an extension of himself. He had relied absolutely on the second mate's skill with a boat. And now Dick the trusted, Dick the audacious, Dick the consummate mariner . . . a momentary inattention, no more! He, Bride, had been powerless to alter the course of the event.

The master forced his mind from its study of cause and effect. There was no profit in it. Wasteful, or folly, to grub in the past. None of it could be retrieved. There was work to be done.

He lifted his binoculars, fixed them on the boat. He stared in unwilling admiration. Here was a paradox. He distrusted that man. The sea in its reckless daring and detachment was not a metaphor of John Driscoll's interior landscape. The man was elusive. He was frangible. He was diminished by Dick King's aura, for Dick had been made of sterner stuff. Yet the fourth, in his turns now across the crests and hollows, was guiding his craft in an exemplary manner.

Soon Driscoll would put about. He knew the drill. Bow-on to the seas: survivors on a line. But, by God, keep them clear of his screw!

The whaleboat toiled skyward, then hung on a curling lip. The bowman cried out. Someone else swore. To a man the crew lowered their heads as the boat careered down, far down, into a sculpted declivity: then soared again, very high, giddily, on the wall of a chasing sea. Driscoll's stomach rose in protest; he tasted bile.

The wreck stood off to leeward. Driscoll twisted round, measuring the waves. They moved in tall ranks, and in the foaming troughs the water was black as night shot through with glitter. He judged the seas, he judged them well: letting them surge under him: steering across the seas at a fine angle: calling out from time to time to Mr. Cole to retard the throttle, to keep the boat moving more slowly than the seas.

The seas moved fast beneath the boat, not trapping it or tumbling it, and the waves ran harmlessly out from under.

23

The fourth mate's face reddened in the gray of the boat's world. His pores had come open and the sweat dried coldly in the wind. He pushed the helm or pulled it toward him, keeping the seas on his port quarter. Though the boat yawed, the screw stayed planted, and he kept control even as the motion sickened him, stayed in his throat. Forward, the engineer, bowman and rowers-in-reserve gauged his every move. They were dependent, not adoring. They sat in judgment. And as he met their gaze he concentrated on the sea. Absorbed in the steering, he had damped an impulse to flight. He had mastered the boat. He had become purposeful, resolute. He wielded the tiller as he would a sturdy ax. Those quivering slopes were the enemy. They rushed insolently by in a jolt and tremor along his hull. He would vanquish them.

At the peak of a climb he could see the wreck three crests off. It was poised, motionless. It vanished into a trough.

Come across smartly, he told himself. Do not get trapped against the wreck. He must not do that. His boat was a trifling thing. Stand in close but do not get trapped.

With a shove of the helm he turned the boat parallel to the low side of the wreck, the boat mounting a spacious hill.

"Stand off!" The bowman's voice was shrill with alarm. Driscoll took no notice. There was room enough. He would move in close, closer still.

"Have a care, mister," shouted the engineer. "You'll have us aboard."

The whaleboat heeled and the lunatic rollers lifted under, the seas carrying the boat down on the wreck. The two vessels threatened to join. They came apart. The bowman fingered a coil of line. He looked aft. Driscoll held him with his eyes. "When I tell you . . . steady, steady . . . not before. . . ." The boat rocked to within yards of the hulk's weather bulwarks. The bowman practice swung the weighted rope. Feet and knees in the forewell, he braced himself against the rolling and stretched his throwing arm in a curve that went far behind his back.

The whaleboat moved fast up the weather side of the wreck. On the back curl of a rising sea it found the wind. The men of *Achilles* had got up now, all except the boy. They held to the lee coaming of Number Three. In the boat the bowman looked back imploringly at the fourth mate, as if his line was a burden too heavy to bear. He had to be rid of it. Then, from Driscoll: "Now!" Instantly the bowman's arm scythed round in a blur. The line sailed on the wind, carried in a pretty arc, snagged high on the wreck's sheltering hatch. Carpenter Fiddle threw himself forward—he had it.

Driscoll pushed the tiller alee. The boat sheered off; came up into the shadowing waves.

24

Hand over hand the bowman paid out the line. Made fast to its end, and lashed round a bundle of kapok, ran a length of stout cordage. This, too, slipped over the side. As it did, Driscoll kept the little boat a point or two off the seas. With the throttle retarded he neither lost nor gained way. Nicely balanced, the cockleshell shouldered into the waves.

Well to leeward, the *City of Tampa* gamboled about. Vast pyramids and basaltic domes exposed her to view, then swallowed her whole. And into this nether precinct of heaving, fretting gray a white bird flew: lured to the ship by some imperative of inner navigation: divining perhaps an omen of land in the liner's belching funnel.

From his perch upwind Driscoll regarded the bird and the vessel's scattering smoke. He was cheered by that smoke. A solid hull lay beneath it. But his eyes, lingering on those charcoal drifts, were brought back with a start by some color hard by. On the wave-washed wreck a man stirred. It was Carpenter Fiddle. He had encased himself in orange. The bowman's thick three-strand encircled his waist. Moving now, descending the incline forward of the hatch, he trod delicately, like a dancer on ice—a misstep would have pitched him athwart. He slid one foot forward; he slid the other. He toed over wire. He took his time about it. No need to rush. Downhill, seas cascaded on deck. Here and there a bit of bulwarks rose clear like flotsam in a tiderace. Beyond, the carpenter conjectured, lay a watery tomb.

Driscoll, in the offing, observing the sliding man, had become more and more sure of himself in the work of guiding the boat. He was strong and exultant. His sinews had gone taut as bowstrings; his nausea had passed. Once again, death would not touch him. He stood with the living: invincible; indestructible; heroic.

The mood ebbed. Arrogance gave way to irony. As Driscoll watched Fiddle's peculiar glissade, the notion came to him that he as much as that fumbling acrobat was a survivor of sorts: that what he had accomplished in the boat was the essence of survival: proof of triumph over terror. But his proof lacked conviction. It glowed like a tepid spark. It had no virtue. It was absurd. He had proved a specific of fortitude: he had proved nothing. His courage was chimerical. It was a thing of the imagination. It proclaimed itself like Chanticleer, yet his wretchedness had not been exorcised. What he had done would not endure. It would have to be done again, for right conduct had a certain periodic importance (if pressed, though, he could not have told you why—one's refusals to poke about the opaque shadows of extinction were as often shrugged off, or supported in torment until time drove them from memory).

He brooded: courage was vanity; pity was egoism. They were a dreamer's indulgence. He considered the pointlessness of action in the face of his deceit. What did it matter to him if those devils on *Achilles* lived or died. . . .

"Look alive!" Mr. Cole exclaimed. The engineer flung out a hand—the bow had fallen off; the boat drifted downsea—and his reproachful eyes prodded the fourth mate's oblivion.

Driscoll thumped the tiller, brought the craft's head up a point. He turned the false mask of savior on the wreck and waited for the sliding man to go over the side.

25

The wind had freshened. With it came gusts of snow. The men in the boat bent their heads against the wind, which struck them with terrible force and whipped the green-black sea to a frenzy of spume. Driscoll kept position by the feel of the boat, for the snow, carried on the wind, stung his eyes. Involuntary tears coursed down his cheeks. Then the snow blew off to leeward and the wind fell again.

Aboard the wreck the sliding man waited for his chance. As the gusts died, he dropped to the flooded crotch between deck and bulwarks. The ocean carried him free. He gasped from the cold of it. To his surprise, the kapok kept him afloat.

"Ay-yoh!" chanted the men of the boat in unison, pulling on

the line. Soon diligent hands reached into the sea. They clutched Carpenter Fiddle by a tie of his kapok. Heaving up hard, the men rolled him over the gunwale onto a side bench. Water ran from his ears and mouth. His eyes were glazed; his neck lay askew like a rubbery stalk.

The bowman struck him across the face. He aimed another blow, this one more violent. The carpenter coughed convulsively and sat up.

Driscoll, gripping the tiller, looked dully at the faces of the men in the boat, gleaming with spray and melting snow; and at the face of the carpenter, purple and red from the bowman's resuscitating blows. His own face had a piratical air. His parched and gelid lower lip had split; blood flowed copiously. The bowman and the engineer stared at him askance. They feared his wildness. His eyes had become transfigured by the wind and snow, and there was a hint of madness, or of cruelty, in those fevered slits and hooded lids.

It occurred to Driscoll that his mouth tasted of salt, a gall not of the sea. His gloved hand came away bloody from his chin. He looked down at the stain with curiosity, but it did not trouble him. He seemed purged of sensation. He thought no more about vanity and egoism. He thought now about nothing. He turned his face back to the wreck.

The boat dipped into a hollow; it sped to a summit. There was a splash—it was seen from the crest—and the boatmen hauled on the line. Their shoulders strained to the task. A pair of swimmers tossed in the sea. They were Mr. Rowe and Joe Corcum. Mr. Rowe hurled an arm about. His other—the fist of it—was entangled in the boy's hair. And without that uphold-ing fist the head of the boy, who provided no assistance, who made no effort to help himself, would surely have gone under.

The men of the boat snared the newcomers—dragged them rudely onto the forward thwarts. Mr. Rowe blew and flopped like a fish. The boy lay mute, unmoving. A brownish ooze stained his tattered trouser leg; it mingled with the drench of seawater, puddling the bilge.

The bowman covered the boy with a blanket.

"Well?" called Driscoll.

The bowman shook his head.

"Is he dead?"

"I don't know," the bowman said.

It did not matter. There was no time for reflection. One more trophy played on the line. This one swam desperately even as the boatmen towed him through the waves, for the swimmer would leave nothing to chance. Brought alongside, then beached, he smelt of diesel oil. His immersion in water had not washed it away. He was Mr. McCabe, the chief engineer.

"Bless you, lads!"

The boat vaulted from crest to abyss, and to crest again: the men silent.

The line stretched and twanged. The next to slide onto a thwart was the last, the master: his very grimness bespoke command, or lost command. The bowman pulled in a bit of trailing line and Driscoll put up the helm. The cockleshell fell off downwind.

Driscoll had the rollers now on his stern. Over his shoulder he could see them curl and foam. But the boat rode easily enough. He looked to leeward. Across the illimitable peaks and valleys, the *City of Tampa* heeled in erratic arcs. The ship was laying down oil: she would subdue the tumult around her.

Joe Corcum continued up the dingy road. The young Thameside brawler peered behind; peered ahead. His spunk had failed him. No place to be this time of night. He wandered past grimy brick facings: a bleak and murderous thoroughfare where lamplight glimmered, filtered through fog. He had drunk his fill of Bass, and a good piss-up it was. He had danced clockwise round a ballroom oval with a girl from the north, from a place called Bootle. She had kissed him wetly on the lips. . . .

Now as he groped his way up Wapping High Street his eyes were skittish with fright. He stumbled over a marauding tom. His heart beat more loudly against complaining ribs. On past Old Stairs, Gun Wharf, New Crane Wharf . . . up toward his mum's, in Wapping Wall. . . .

An indeterminate shape rose up out of the dark. It accosted him. It enfolded him like a cloak. He shook himself free. He stood ready to strike.

"Come on, come on, damn it!" he called out in a weak, panicky voice. Water seemed to lap up round him. That was queer. He was cold, wet: no use trying to get warm. The idea amused him and he tried to laugh, but his mouth had stiffened in a rictus. His lips, gray and encrusted with salt, stretched wide over stained teeth. Something bitter rose in his throat. He kicked his good leg from side to side.

The boy had been lifted from the thwarts to a wider side bench. Captain Tyrrel stroked his brow. "Don't be afraid, lad," he said. Joe Corcum breathed heavily, eyes closed. Suddenly he spoke with animation: "Not afraid, not afraid!" Then he was silent. He turned his head and vomited blood.

Tyrrel called to him: "Joe, do you hear me? It's me, lad. Do you hear?" The boy opened his eyes. They bulged from skeletal chambers. The boy began to breathe in shallow draughts. Soon his breathing stopped.

26

Far downsea the whaleboat came round the *Tampa's* lee. It beat its way forward, flinging spray. The fourth mate sagged against the tiller. A kneeling man bowed over a recumbent form.

On the liner's bridge, Captain Bride followed the boat's capers with vacant eyes. He felt neither elation nor satisfaction, but indifference coupled with the dregs of his anger. The cockleshell had the look of unreality about it and he himself might have been a fraud. He was estranged from that fragile craft. His ship alone was certain and safe. He would withdraw into the wheelhouse, his beloved cocoon. But first the hellish boat must be brought alongside.

Despite the oil he had put down, his ship rolled violently, seas abeam. The master shifted his gaze to the boat deck: to the empty davits of Number One. There could be no possibility of hooking on.

The chief mate stood within earshot.

"Let the boat go," Bride said. "Bring them up the nets." He gestured vaguely. "That injured seaman, mister. More likely dead. They'll give us a line. . . ."

The mate went off. Bride resumed his sea vigil. High above his head a flag halyard chattered: the wind to port was getting up again. The combers spilled in chalky folds. A squall of snow billowed out of the northwest. Soon the ship was in it. The steam whistle blared.

Driscoll lifted his head to the basso call. It came to him like a clarion of reprieve. Through the murk and driving snow he could make out the outline of funnel and superstructure; but the sea, though bound by oil, was large with a heavy surge. A signal lamp blinked.

"Do you read?" said Mr. Cole.

Driscoll moved his lips in synchrony to the rhythmic glim.

"Into the nets . . . leave this. . . ."

Driscoll took comfort from the flickering lamp. There was life behind that piercing eye. Rapt in its promise of warmth and light, he had forgotten the boy. The spell was broken by a disjointed thought. It was insistent. Driscoll regarded the still figure.

"Get a line on him," he called forward.

"Not a pretty sight," Mr. McCabe said.

The bowman gave a short, nervous laugh: "He'll keep on ice."

Cole raised a threatening fist.

The bowman drew back in a sulk. He busied himself with a length of line, and made fast a bight round the boy's chest.

Driscoll steered for the sound of the horn. The snow blinded him. He was weak in the limbs. The boat careered on its course through a fantastic sea. Once again the boat battered his body and spirit. The cockleshell fell away; it rose and lurched. As the snow drove down on the wind, Driscoll held up a hand to ward off its sting. He lowered his head. The heads of the boatmen were lowered, too. The snow matted their lifejackets and caps. The castaways of *Achilles* huddled in blankets. They swayed from cold and fatigue. Someone muttered a prayer. The voice Driscoll heard was Isabel's. *Remember me*, the voice said. A tongue of guilt darted from memory.

He was weary. He wished to rest. Exhausted by despair, he would sleep. He thought it was time to do that. Perhaps he would do that. Perhaps he would drink of that vessel where there no longer would be terror, or melancholy and madness, or remorse, or desire.

Mechanically Driscoll heaved on the tiller, keeping his bow a point or two off the sea. He must not let the boat fall off too far. He must hold her close. The trumpeting horn urged him on.

The body of the boy rocked on the bench with the motion of the boat. In a lull, the snow blowing clear, Driscoll could see him plain. The cheeks were blanched, the eyebrows frosted. There was neither hope nor deliverance in that childlike face. There was no repose. He himself must look much that way. The boy was the shade that touched his imagination. Driscoll's mind rebelled against nullity. There was no good wishing for that.

After a while he calmed himself. And so it was beginning to go now. It would not touch him. He did not think he would be touched by it.

The litany of familiar deceit came to him in solace. In the enclosure of the boat the fourth mate attended the helm.

Alfred, New York—Martel, France—Athens, Greece